The Tyler Twins:
Surprise at Big Key Ranch

The Tyler Twins:
Surprise at
Big Key Ranch

Hilda Stahl

Tyndale House Publishers, Inc. Wheaton, Illinois

Other books by Hilda Stahl

The Tyler Twins Series
1 Surprise at Big Key Ranch
2 The Swamp Monster
3 Pet Show Panic
4 Latchkey Kids
5 Treehouse Hideaway
6 The Missing Grandfather

The Elizabeth Gail Series
1 Elizabeth Gail and the Mystery at the Johnson Farm
2 Elizabeth Gail and the Secret Box
3 Elizabeth Gail and the Teddy Bear Mystery
4 Elizabeth Gail and the Dangerous Double
5 Elizabeth Gail and Trouble at Sandhill Ranch
6 Elizabeth Gail and the Strange Birthday Party
7 Elizabeth Gail and the Terrifying News
8 Elizabeth Gail and the Frightened Runaways
9 Elizabeth Gail and Trouble from the Past
10 Elizabeth Gail and the Silent Piano
11 Elizabeth Gail and Double Trouble
12 Elizabeth Gail and the Holiday Mystery
13 Elizabeth Gail and the Missing Love Letters
14 Elizabeth Gail and the Music Camp Romance
15 Elizabeth Gail and the Handsome Stranger
16 Elizabeth Gail and the Secret Love
17 Elizabeth Gail and the Summer for Weddings
18 Elizabeth Gail and the Time for Love

Cover and interior illustration copyright © 1990 by Rick Johnson

Juvenile trade paper edition

ISBN 0-8423-7631-3
Printed in the United States of America

96 95 94 93 92 91 90
8   7   6   5   4   3   2   1

CONTENTS

ONE: Terryl's Great Plan   7

TWO: Lost at the Airport   13

THREE: Mom's News   23

FOUR: Three Dogs   31

FIVE: The Keyes Family   39

SIX: The Birthday Party   49

SEVEN: A Talk with Mom   59

EIGHT: Sarah James   69

NINE: Sunday Surprises   77

TEN: The Ice Storm   85

ELEVEN: The Terrible Fight   95

TWELVE: The Missing Photograph   105

THIRTEEN: Broken Plants   113

FOURTEEN: Happy Family   119

ONE
Terryl's Great Plan

Terryl Tyler stopped dead in the hallway, pressed her lips together, and frowned. Anger darkened her brown eyes and made her heart thud so loud she thought Dad and Briana Jarvis could hear it. How dare Briana come to visit Dad today of all days, when she and her twin sister, Pam, were leaving for nine months to live with Mom? Briana knew she wasn't welcome—except by Dad, maybe, because she was tall and very beautiful and hung on him as if she loved him.

Terryl's stomach tightened and she gripped the handle of her violin case tighter. She didn't want Dad and Briana to fall in love and get married. It was bad enough to know that Mom had married some terrible stranger named David Keyes. Terryl shivered and tears stung her eyes.

"We'll have dinner at seven," Terryl heard Dad say in a soft voice that sent jealousy raging through her. "I have to catch a plane to New York at ten."

"I could go with you, Richard darling." Briana slipped her arms around his waist and smiled into his dark eyes. It made Terryl sick and she almost turned away to go back to the bedroom she shared with Pam.

"I thought you had a modeling job in the morning," Richard said, cupping her face in his hands. Briana was wearing two-inch heels, so they were the same height. Terryl studied the contrast they presented; Dad had dark hair and eyes and Briana had red hair and green eyes. "How about if you join me in New York on Sunday?" Terryl's dad said to Briana.

She laughed softly. "I'd like that."

"So would I." He kissed her and Terryl spun around on the plush carpet and ran to the bedroom, her violin case bumping her leg.

Pam looked up from where she sat on the carpeted floor. "What'd Dad say about taking your violin?" She thought it was dumb for Terryl to bother with violin during the nine months with Mom when Dad wasn't around to force her to practice. But then, Pam wasn't like Terryl and music didn't interest her the way it did her twin.

Terryl flung the violin onto her bed, on top of the piles of clothes that she'd decided not to take to Mom's. "I didn't ask him about it! *She's* here."

Pam frowned as she pushed herself up, leaving the stuffed animals on the floor around her feet. She'd been trying to decide what to take and what to leave. Nine months was a long time to be without one of her friends. "Briana is here? Today? She knows we have to go to the airport soon." Pam pushed back her long honey-brown hair with a trembling hand. "She won't go with us, will she?"

"Who knows what she'll do!" Terryl flung out her arms. "Who knows what anyone will do anymore."

Pam turned away to hide her flush. It always

embarrassed her when Terryl got so dramatic.

Terryl flipped back her honey-brown hair and lifted her round chin defiantly. "I think it's terrible, Pamela."

"What is?" Pam asked as she picked up the stuffed animals and set them neatly on the shelves near her bed. She might as well leave them all here since she had others at Mom's. But maybe it would be different now since Mom lived at the Big Key Ranch with that man. A shiver ran up and down Pam's spine.

"That we don't have any control over any part of our lives. Here we are ten years old, going on eleven, and we have to do exactly what Mom, Dad, and the court say!"

Pam frowned. "We just turned ten today, September first, and all the kids we know have to obey their parents and the court's ruling if their parents are divorced."

"I suppose it doesn't bother you at all to go live with Mom and that man! Or I suppose you could just stay here with Dad even if he married Briana, the model." Terryl struck a model's pose and pranced across the bedroom in an exaggerated model's walk. "I guess nothing really bothers you, does it, Pam? You live every day just the way you're ordered to without any questions, without really caring what happens to you."

Pam bit her lower lip and forced back the tight lump in her throat. "What else can we do? We have to stay with Mom nine months and with Dad three months." She hated it when Terryl forced her to think about their way of life. Before the divorce they'd all lived together here in Detroit in this plush apartment and Terryl hadn't poked and pushed to make her notice what was going on around her.

Terryl shook her head with a frown. Pam was too easygoing, too ready to fall in with whatever anyone wanted her to do. "We'll have to do something to make them all stop to think about us for a change!"

"Don't do anything terrible, Terryl."

"Me? What makes you think I will?"

Pam pushed her suitcase closer to the closed bedroom door. "In another hour we're going to be on a plane to Grand Rapids. You don't have time to try anything."

Terryl walked to the window and looked out over the city, her brain whirling with ideas. Finally she spun around. "I know what we'll do!"

Pam sank into the chair near her desk. She knew by the look on her twin's face that she wasn't going to like the idea.

Terryl tugged her shirt over her jeans and her eyes sparkled with mischief. "You and I are not going to Grand Rapids today! We are going to take our things that we have packed and we are going to sneak over to Grandmother's."

Pam's heart sank. She knew there was no way she could talk Terryl out of her plan. "Grandmother's not home today."

"That's even better!" Terryl grinned and clasped her hands together in front of herself. "She won't be there to call Dad and tell him where we are. It's a perfect plan, Pam. We'll sneak away as soon as we can and Dad won't be able to find us. That way,

Mom won't be able to blame him when we don't get to Grand Rapids. Then, when Grandmother gets home, we'll convince her that it's in our best interest to let us stay with her. She's always saying that Dad should do things that are in our best interest."

Pam locked her fingers together in her lap. "What if we can't sneak away? What if Dad is always close to us?" Pam didn't want to sneak away; she wanted to see Mom again after three long months with Dad. She felt closest to Mom and Terryl felt closest to Dad. Pam wanted to be with Mom again, even if she *was* married to that man.

Terryl shook her head. "Dad can't be with us every minute, can he? And even if he is, we'll find a way to sneak away from him even if we have to wait until we get to the airport." It would serve Dad right to have them disappear. Maybe then he'd forget about Briana.

Just then the door opened and Dad stepped in. Terryl flushed with guilt and Pam ducked her head, pretending to study the ring that Dad had given her for her birthday.

"Are you girls ready?" Richard asked, then he frowned. "You are not going dressed in jeans. We already discussed this."

"I don't want to put on that suit, Dad." Terryl wrinkled her nose at the red skirt and jacket draped over the foot of her bed. Pam had an identical suit on her bed. "We want to wear jeans."

Richard shook his head. "You girls are going dressed properly. I want you to put on your suits and new shoes and come right out so we can leave."

"Is it time already?" Terryl forced back the panic she felt. "We don't have to be at the airport until one."

"I'm taking you out to lunch." He picked up their suitcases and started for the door. "I'll give you both five minutes." He smiled over his shoulder. "Hurry, please. I have a surprise waiting for you."

Terryl dropped to the bed, her chin in her hands. "I hope Briana's not the surprise."

Pam pulled off her tee shirt and jeans. "I guess we won't be able to sneak away to Grandmother's."

Terryl leaped up, her dark eyes flashing. "Oh, yes, we will! We'll find a way, Pamela."

Terryl dressed slowly, her mind whirling with brilliant ideas on ways to escape. She had to find a way to make Dad pay for getting the divorce and for daring to consider making Briana their new mother.

A great sadness rose up inside Terryl and tears blurred her vision as she looked in the mirror to brush her hair.

Pam's heart also sank as she dressed in the red suit and white blouse with red trim. She pushed her feet into the shoes that hurt her right heel. *I should just tell Terryl to forget the plan,* she thought. But she knew she wouldn't. Terryl knew just what to say to make her cry, and today on their tenth birthday, she didn't want to cry. She wanted to get to Grand Rapids to see Mom, to feel Mom's arms around her again. If only everything wasn't so messed up!

TWO
Lost at the Airport

Terryl gripped her blue nylon duffel bag that she
was to carry on the plane with her and flipped back
her long honey-brown hair. The taste of the beautiful
birthday cake at lunch was still with her. It had
been hard to eat only a few bites, but she didn't
want Dad to know it had pleased her. She wanted to
force him to find a way for them all to live together
again as a family, a happy family.

The airport crowd pressed against her and she
bumped against Pam, who turned to smile at her
nervously. It was like looking in a mirror. After ten
years Terryl was used to being and having an
identical twin, but people around them stared and
nudged each other and pointed. Terryl ignored
them. "Let's go," she mouthed to Pam.

Pam's heart sank as she shot a look at Dad just as
he picked up the airline tickets that would take
them across the state to Mom. Pam turned back to
Terryl and forced herself to nod. She'd been hoping
Terryl would give up the idea of sneaking away to
Grandmother's.

Pam's gray nylon duffel bag suddenly felt too
heavy and she changed hands. Her stomach
tightened in fear. What would Dad do when they

disappeared? She shivered and closed her dark eyes for a moment, wondering how she would find the strength to follow Terryl.

Terryl eased out of the long waiting line, hesitated to make sure Pam was right behind her, then strode toward the wide stairs that she knew led to restrooms. The noise rose around her and enveloped her and she knew Dad wouldn't notice the click of her new shoes on the tile.

"Not so fast, Terryl." Pam's voice was urgent and Terryl glanced back with an impatient frown. "My shoe hurts my heel."

"Forget the pain, Pam. Once we're in the restroom you can change into your tennies." Terryl waited for the feel of Dad's eyes boring into her back. She'd know if he spotted them just as she knew when Pam wanted her before she said anything. They both could tell when they wanted each other, no matter how far apart they were. Mom had said that came with being twins. Terryl's stomach tightened painfully. She didn't want to think about Mom right now; she wanted to zigzag through the crowd to get away from Dad, but she knew Pam couldn't keep up.

Pam bit her bottom lip and forced herself to look straight ahead and not peek back to see if Dad was watching them. A hand gripped her arm and she squealed, then sighed in relief when she saw it was her twin. "You scared me."

"You have to hurry, Pam. We have to change and get outside to catch a taxi before Dad finds us." Terryl darted a look around for an average-sized man dressed in a gray wool suit and black shoes you could see yourself in, carrying a briefcase that held the second draft of the detective novel he was writing.

Did he carry the divorce papers in a special compartment in his case? Was he glad that they weren't a family any longer? It didn't seem to bother him at all to know that Mom lived across the state. Maybe one of these days he'd tell Mom to keep them with her always so that he could be free to travel as he wanted and marry who he wanted without any hassle.

Terryl swallowed hard and ducked around two old ladies that reminded her of Grandmother. Dad wouldn't ever give her up, would he? She loved him so much she ached inside when she had to leave him. He loved her, too; he'd said so many times. But once he'd told Mom that he loved her, too, and that love had died. Maybe a father's love for a daughter could die just like a husband's love for a wife. And if he did marry Briana or some other woman, Terryl was sure it could easily happen.

Pam clutched at her sister's arm. "Please, let's go back to Dad." It had taken all of Pam's courage to say it, but now that she had, she was glad. "I want to see Mom again, don't you?"

Terryl did. If she had to choose between her parents, she knew she couldn't, not when she loved them both so much. "This plan will make them do something to make *us* happy, Pam," Terryl said firmly. "It'll make Dad find a way so that we can live with both of them again."

Pam shook her head. "But Mom's married, Terryl."

"Then she'll just have to get unmarried!" Terryl pushed Pam ahead of her into the restroom. "Hurry up and change. Dad will never think to look for two girls in jeans. And be sure to wear that baseball cap with your hair tucked up inside like I told you."

Pam didn't have the nerve to argue. Tears blurred her vision as she walked around two teenage girls and a woman dressed in a short black dress. Inside the small stall she pulled off her suit and slipped on jeans, a blue tee shirt, and tied the comfortable white and blue Nikes on her feet. She shoved the suit and blouse and slip into the duffel bag and tugged on the blue baseball cap that Terryl had bought when they had talked about playing softball with the other kids in their apartment building. She shivered as she picked up her bag and walked out of the stall. Would she ever learn to stand up to Terryl and disagree with her?

Terryl laughed as she looked at Pam. "Dad will never recognize us now, as long as we don't get close to him." Terryl tucked the locket that held pictures of herself and Pam when they were a year old inside her tee shirt and motioned for Pam to do the same.

Dad was great on detail. When he sent the security people looking for them he'd describe his daughters as twins with flowing honey-brown hair that reached halfway down their slender backs, who were dressed in matching red suits with white blouses and gold lockets. Now, however, Terryl wore a black short-sleeve sweatshirt that her friend Jim had left at the apartment when he was there playing with the computer. Dad would never in a million years recognize her if he did happen to see her before they left the terminal.

Maybe, after a few days of them being missing, Dad and Mom would straighten out their lives. Maybe they would find a way that she and Pam could have a mom and dad who lived together again, instead of a dad who lived in Detroit in a fancy apartment, and a mom who lived on a ranch near Grand Rapids.

The thought of horses and living on a real ranch sent excitement bubbling inside her, but she forced it away angrily. So what if there were horses? So what if Mom had said she'd teach them to ride? That wouldn't stop Terryl from trying to get their family back together. Even if Mom was married again, things could work out if they all wanted them to.

"I'm ready," whispered Pam as she lifted her gray bag.

Terryl took a deep breath. "Me, too."

Together they walked out of the restroom and toward the wide stairs. Soon they'd be outdoors and in a taxi. Several minutes later Pam caught Terryl's arm. "Shouldn't we be to the outside doors by now?" Terryl looked around with a frown, but couldn't find the heavy glass doors.

They stopped beside the revolving advertisement for a large business. How could they miss the doors? There were lots of them and they slid open when you reached them. Had they taken the wrong turn out of the restrooms?

"Are we lost?" whispered Pam, her dark eyes wide with fright.

17

"I don't know."

"We could ask someone what to do."

Terryl frowned and shook her head. "We don't want anyone to notice us. We don't want Dad to find us." An icy band tightened around her heart. Could she really do this to Dad, He would be terrified when he realized they were missing. She lifted her chin and gripped her duffel bag tighter. It was all his fault anyway. He was the one who had wanted the divorce. He'd said that Mom would always stay a small-time country girl, and he had grown into a professional big-time writer with different tastes than hers.

Mom had been glad to walk away from Detroit and go to a small place in the country. It had tired her to keep up with Dad, tired and angered her. She had begged Dad for years to move to the country so the twins could have a yard and animals, but he had refused. He was a city boy and she was a country girl, and their love for each other had died during their fights over their life-styles.

Pam looked around fearfully for anyone that looked wicked enough to steal identical twin girls, but everyone looked normal. That didn't make her feel any better and she moved closer to Terryl. "Let's ask that man over there with the blue uniform on."

Terryl shook her head. "We'll find our way, Pam." Then she noticed a big red-haired man watching them and her heart hammered painfully. He walked toward them. If he dared to touch her she'd scream loud enough for Mom to hear her at Big Key Ranch!

The man walked past and she breathed easier. She turned slowly, eyes narrowing as she studied her surroundings. "Let's go that way, Pam. I think that's the way to the door."

"Are you sure?"

"No, but we'll try it."

They walked around groups of laughing, talking people, and dodged out of the way of people rushing to reach their planes. Finally they stopped near a large planter and Terryl drew a ragged breath. Who would've thought they would get lost trying to find a way out of the airport?

Suddenly a strong hand gripped her arm and she shrieked. She looked up as she pulled away, then froze as her eyes locked with her dad's. Fire shot from his dark eyes and she trembled.

Pam moved slightly and he caught her arm and held her in place. She bit her lower lip and stared at the floor dismally.

"Just what do you girls think you're doing?" He demanded as he eyed them up and down. "Why did you run away from me and why did you change your clothes?"

Pam pulled into herself and the color drained from her face. She hated to be yelled at. Terryl, however, lifted her chin half defiantly. "We are not going to stay with Mom! We are going to live with Grandmother."

"That's impossible! You must go to your mother now!" Richard looked from one to the other and his anger melted away. "Pretty good disguise, girls. I saw you earlier, but I didn't recognize you at all. I wouldn't have now, but I spotted your ring, Pam."

She flushed painfully and wouldn't meet Terryl's angry look.

"There isn't time to put on your red suits," their dad said with a resigned sigh, "so you'll have to wear your jeans. I wanted you to look nice for your mother."

He quickly led them through the crowds, past the security checkpoint, to their boarding gate.

"Don't make us go, Dad!" Terryl looked up with large, pleading eyes. "We don't want to meet that man she married."

Richard shook his head. "I know it's scary for you, but you must go. I didn't force you to attend the wedding, but now I have no choice." He kissed each one. "Your mother is expecting you and we can't let her down, can we?"

A tear slipped down Pam's pale cheek. She couldn't wait to see Mom again. Would she be different now that she had a new husband?

Terryl lifted her head high, her face set and her shoulders square. She had to go, no matter how she felt. At least she'd have the new violin that Dad had bought her for her birthday. Maybe it was already loaded on the plane. It would help her to forget, for awhile, that her life was messed up.

"See you in nine months, girls." Richard held first Pam and then Terryl close in his arms and kissed them. "I'll call you often, and write."

"'Bye, Dad," whispered Pam, clinging to his well-shaped hand.

Terryl blinked back tears, embarrassed to think that she might cry the way she had the last time she'd left Dad. "Good-bye," she said just above a whisper. "I hope you finish your book soon."

21

"I will." He kissed her cheek again, then stepped back, his lashes damp with tears.

Terryl turned quickly away and walked with Pam toward the ramp.

THREE
Mom's News

Terryl peeked at her mom and frowned as they drove away from the airport. Mom was no longer Kathleen Tyler, she was Kathleen Keyes, Mrs. David Keyes. *How can Pam just sit in the front seat beside Mom and chatter away as if nothing has happened,* she wondered angrily, *as if nothing was different?*

Mom even looked a little different, and Terryl tried to figure out why. Her wavy dark hair was still medium length. She wore very little make up and was dressed in jeans and a bulky tan sweater with a white shirt underneath, the collar and cuffs peeked out. A plain gold wedding band circled her finger where once she'd worn a diamond engagement ring with a fancy gold wedding band.

"My, but you girls have grown since I saw you last!" she said with a smile. "I'm glad Dad let you wear jeans for the trip."

Terryl looked down at her clenched hands. Mom had said that twice already since she'd met them. Was that the only thing she could say? What about, "Sorry to have messed up your lives, girls. Sorry we're not a family any longer. Sorry I married David Keyes."

Terryl stared out the window as her mother pulled

23

into a park and turned off the ignition. She twisted around to smile at Pam, then Terryl. "Girls, I'm so glad to see you! I just can't get over how you've grown!"

"How come we're stopping here?" asked Pam, waving toward the picnic tables and swing sets. A cool September wind blew across the grass. Pam's stomach cramped. Was Mom going to send them away because she was too busy with her new husband? Maybe she didn't want daughters any longer. Maybe they were a bother to her now that she lived on a ranch the way she'd always wanted.

Kathleen tucked her honey-brown hair behind her ears, and studied her daughters. Her brown eyes held a contented look that Terryl had never seen before. Her cheeks were rosy and she looked younger than she had three months ago. "Girls, I have something I want to tell you, and I wanted to do it while we're still alone."

Terryl moved restlessly, and Pam looked at her mother in concern.

"What is it, Mom?" Pam's voice was low and strained.

Kathleen squeezed Pam's icy hand and smiled, then reached back and patted Terryl's jean-clad knee. "I wanted you to know . . . I am happy for the first time in my entire life, really happy way down inside. But it's not just because of David and his love and living on the Big Key. It's something really, really special." She took a deep breath and moistened her full lips with the tip of her tongue. "Girls, I've learned about God. I know that we've talked about

24

God in the past, about the fact that he created all things. But I've learned that he loves me and he loves you and that he sent Jesus here to earth to die on the cross for us so that we could have a close relationship with God.

"When sin came into the world it made God sad. He wanted to find a way to bring all of us close to himself again, so he sent Jesus, his Son. Jesus died on the cross, but he didn't stay dead. He fought a battle with Satan and won and then came back to life and went to heaven to be with his Father."

The words were foreign to Terryl, but she could see that Mom was excited about what she was saying. She seemed to have a special bond with God that she'd never had before. Watching and listening to her made Terryl feel strange inside.

Pam nodded and slowly relaxed. She knew what Mom was talking about. She'd heard a man on TV talking about God as her heavenly Father and Jesus as her Savior and Lord and friend. She had wanted to pray with the man, but she'd hesitated. She'd forgotten all about it until now.

"Girls, I have an inner peace that I never had before," Kathleen continued. "I talk to God and he helps me and gives me strength and wisdom and love. I want both of you to discover this same personal relationship that I have with God. I want you both to experience the peace and love that comes from knowing God in a personal way. David and Dani both are born again Christians, and so are David's parents."

Terryl frowned. "Who's Dani?" Were they going to have to share Mom with some boy?

Kathleen cleared her throat and Terryl could see she was a little nervous. "I didn't tell you about Dani in my letters because I wanted to do it in person. Dani is David's ten-year-old daughter. You girls have a new sister and I know you'll learn to love her as much as I do."

The girls sat in stunned silence.

"Her name is Danelle, but we call her Dani. She's looking forward to meeting both of you."

The girls stared at Kathleen with wide, horrified looks. Traffic sounds from the street in front of the park seeped through the closed windows. Mom's perfume suddenly seemed too sticky sweet and Terryl rolled her window down for a gulp of fresh air. As the chilly September breeze rushed in she breathed easier. Pam tucked her hair behind her ears with shaking hands.

"You also have new grandparents that you'll meet and love. You'll call them Gran and Grandad. They live at the ranch, too."

Pam hunched into herself, her face drawn and pale. How could she get used to so many new people all at once? Would she have to share a bedroom with Dani as well as with Terryl? She thought of Dad's two-bedroom apartment and the tiny apartment that Mom had had before she married the stranger, and she shuddered. How would so many people fit into one house?

Terryl leaned back and closed her eyes, trying to shut out Mom and the pictures she was drawing of the people on the ranch. How could Mom put them in such a terrible situation? How could she expect them to live together with so many strangers? Why

26

hadn't she begged harder to stay with Dad, or tried harder to escape to Grandmother? Suddenly Terryl thought of something. She leaned forward. "Mom, what do we call your new husband?"

Kathleen sat very still. "I would like you to call him Dad."

"No!" Terryl shook her head hard.

"No," whispered Pam.

Kathleen looked at them, and tears glistened in her eyes. "Oh, girls, I just want you to be happy! I want you to learn to love your new family, and I want you to learn to love God." She sighed and smiled shakily. "I won't make you call David Dad. You can call him David. He won't mind. He'll love you no matter what." She turned on the ignition key. "Let's go to the Big Key now, shall we?"

"Do we have to?" Terryl muttered, folding her arms over her thin chest and pushing out her chin.

"Terryl, give yourself a chance to enjoy your new home." Kathleen said as she pulled onto the street. "It'll take us about fifteen minutes to get there from town."

"Can't we go to your apartment instead?" asked Pam.

"I don't have an apartment now. I gave it up when I married David."

"I'm not going to like him, Mom." Terryl screwed up her face in a terrible scowl. "I won't like him at all! And I won't like his family."

Kathleen shot her a look that made her bite back any further words.

They rode in silence along the tree-lined road. They passed several houses and a few barns. A

27

driver in a red pickup honked and waved at Kathleen and she waved back. Terryl shook her head; nobody in the city honked and waved that way. Cattle dotted a hillside and several horses stood near a round pond.

Finally Kathleen slowed the car and turned it into a long, wide drive. "Here we are, girls," she said brightly with pride in her voice. "Welcome to the Big Key, your new home!"

Terryl's eyes widened as she looked at the wide stretch of lawn that led to a huge house. Trees and bushes dotted the yard, but nothing could dwarf the gigantic two-story house that seemed to stretch for a city block. She pulled her eyes away from the house to the barns and other buildings.

Several horses stood in a large pen near one of the barns. Terryl's heart leaped, then she forced a frown. She would not look at or be happy about the horses! Horses wouldn't win her over. Nothing would. She was going to hate being here and she'd do everything she could to let Mom know it so that she'd send her back to Dad before the nine months were up. At least Dad hadn't remarried yet.

Pam locked her icy fingers together in her lap and looked at the horses fearfully. Could she ever learn to ride? Butterflies fluttered in her stomach. Would Mom hate her if she didn't get excited about the ranch and the animals? Pam sucked in her breath. Could she think of anything to say to David or Dani or the new grandparents?

Just then Pam noticed the house and she leaned forward with a gasp. Was it really a house, or a mansion? "Is that your new house, Mom?" Pam's voice cracked and she flushed with embarrassment.

Kathleen laughed breathlessly. "That's it, all right. Isn't it beautiful? I've always dreamed of living in a house like this in the country."

Terryl shot a look at Mom's beaming face, then looked back out the car window. A tall tree in the side yard had a swing hanging from it, and she wondered how it would feel to swing in a swing made with a rope and board instead of chain and plastic.

Kathleen parked outside the five-car garage and three dogs ran to meet her, barking excitedly. Pam's eyes sparkled. She loved dogs and wasn't afraid of them the way she was of horses or big animals that could step on her.

Terryl sat on her hands to keep from jumping out of the car to pet the dogs. "Does David have *three* dogs?" She'd always wanted a dog, just one dog, but never could because Dad wouldn't allow any pets around. He didn't like animals.

Kathleen laughed softly. "Let's get out and I'll introduce you to the dogs."

Pam looked back at Terryl to see what she was going to do. Terryl frowned, then shrugged as if to say she didn't know how to handle this new situation. Pam turned around and slowly opened the car door. Terryl reached for her jacket, her hands suddenly icy. They were at the Big Key, their new home for the next nine months.

four
Three Dogs

Slowly Terryl slipped from the car and stood beside Pam on the graveled drive. Birds sang in the trees, a horse whinnied, and a cow mooed. The crow of the rooster made Terryl realize she really was in the country with live animals all around her. It wasn't a dream. Oh, it was going to be hard to hate the Big Key!

Kathleen slipped an arm around each girl and hugged them close. "Girls, I want to give you your birthday presents now. I want this to be a very happy birthday for you both." She kissed Pam, then Terryl. "Come meet the dogs. They are special to us."

Kathleen knelt beside the smallest dog, whose black coat looked glossy and healthy. "This is Sugar and she's a cocker spaniel." Then she slipped her arms around a gold and white collie. "This is Lassie, named after the famous collie. She belongs to Dani and has for five years." Kathleen turned to the third dog and rested her hand on his giant hairy head. "And this huge fellow is an Old English sheepdog that I named Malcom because it sounds like such an English name." Kathleen laughed and her cheeks flushed prettily. She reached over and tugged on Sugar's collar. "Pam, this is your birthday gift. Sugar belongs to you."

Pam gasped, then dropped to her knees and hugged the black spaniel. "Oh, Mom, thank you! I can't believe Sugar is mine!"

Terryl watched Sugar and Pam together and her hands itched to stroke the dog herself. Then Kathleen rubbed Malcom's shaggy back. "Terryl, Malcom is your birthday gift. Happy birthday, honey."

Terryl's mouth dropped open as she stared at the black and white sheepdog. Now he was a *real* dog, not a toy like Pam's! Terryl wanted to hug Malcom the way Pam was hugging Sugar, but she held back, her jaw set stubbornly. She felt the look Mom gave her and ignored it.

"I'll get out the luggage while you girls get acquainted with the dogs. Be sure to give Lassie a few pats so she won't feel left out. Dani's still in town with friends and won't be home for another hour." Kathleen unlocked the trunk and lifted out the luggage, handling the violin with great care. "Dani wanted to go to the airport with me, but I told her I wanted time alone with you both."

Terryl inched closer to Malcom, then barely touched the top of the huge head. Malcom leaned against her, almost knocking her off balance. She stared down at him with wide eyes—he liked her. He really did!

Pam chattered happily first to Sugar, then to Lassie. She didn't want Lassie to feel left out. She glanced at Terryl and Malcom and shook her head.

With her arms around Sugar, she whispered, "I'm glad you're mine. I wouldn't want a big dog like Terryl's." Pam rubbed Sugar's long wavy ears and laughed softly. It was going to be all right here on the Big Key after all. She glanced at Terryl and the smile faded. At least, it would be all right as long as Terryl didn't think up some terrible plan for them to run away, or worse.

"Could you girls tear yourselves away from the dogs long enough to help carry in your luggage?" Kathleen laughed happily as she stood beside the cases with her hands at her slender waist and her booted feet apart slightly.

Terryl glanced up and saw how pretty and alive her mom looked. *If Dad saw her now he would fall in love with her all over again,* she thought. But Dad was going to New York to a meeting with his editor and his agent to discuss his new book. He would never take time off to visit the Big Key and see Mom like she was now. With a sigh Terryl gave Malcom one last pat, then walked toward Mom and the luggage.

Just then a blue pickup drove down the long lane toward them. The girls turned to watch, suddenly apprehensive again.

"Here comes David!" Kathleen's face glowed and her voice lilted. "He said he'd get here to meet you both as soon as he could. You'll love him, girls. I know you will!"

Pam inched closer to Terryl and waited with her heart in her mouth. Terryl jammed her hands in her jacket pockets and tried to quiet the wild flutters in her stomach.

The pickup pulled up beside the car and the girls stared at the driver. After he stepped out of the pickup, Terryl's eyes widened in surprise. David was not small and neat like Dad—he was tall and burly with black hair, a nicely trimmed black beard and mustache, and eyes as blue as a summer sky. He wore jeans, Western boots, and a big leather jacket lined with sheepskin.

Terryl glanced at Pam, who gulped. David was a giant! Mom had fallen in love with and married a giant!

Kathleen held her hands out to David and his large hands swallowed hers up. "David," she said, smiling from him to the twins, "this is Pam and this is Terryl."

Terryl knew that once she and Pam changed clothes he'd never be able to tell them apart, and she was glad.

David smiled and his teeth flashed strong and white through his short black beard. "Hello, Pam. Hello, Terryl. I'm happy to meet you both. Welcome to the Big Key."

He didn't try to hug them and Terryl was glad for that. Pam was relieved too, she didn't want him to crack her in half.

"Say hello, girls," said Kathleen stiffly.

"Hello," they said in one tiny voice.

"They like the dogs." Kathleen sounded as if she was forcing the cheerful note in her voice. "They've always wanted a dog. Now we have room for three dogs, four if you count Malcom twice." She laughed and David joined in. The girls stood side by side and looked down at the pavement.

"I hope you girls had a good flight," said David. He slipped a long arm around Kathleen's narrow waist. "The weather is perfect for it." He glanced over his shoulder at the luggage. "You girls can get settled in before Dani, Gran, and Grandad get home to meet you." He easily lifted several suitcases while Kathleen handed Terryl her violin, and Pam the duffel bags.

David's boots clomped heavily on the sidewalk as he walked toward the side door of the huge white house trimmed with black shutters. Kathleen urged the girls to follow him while she walked behind them.

David held the door open and the girls and Kathleen walked into the porch. Jackets hanging on hooks lined the wall; the floor was a cool blue tile and the walls a white paneled wood. A doorway led to a carpeted hallway.

"Wait'll you see your rooms," said Kathleen.

"Rooms?" mouthed Terryl. She had never slept away from Pam. But maybe Mom hadn't meant the rooms to be separate bedrooms for her and Pam.

Pam shrugged and followed David and Mom down the hall to the wide oak stairs that led to another hallway. She looked around to find the house as elaborately decorated as Dad's apartment, only with much more space and many, many more rooms.

"This is Dani's room," said David, nodding toward a closed door. "She's sure looking forward to meeting you two."

Terryl rolled her eyes and made a face and Pam bit back a nervous giggle.

Kathleen opened a door next to Dani's room and stood aside while David walked in with the luggage. He set the cases down and then stood with his hands on his hips and a broad smile on his face.

Terryl looked around at the purple and white bedroom and she frowned. It was gross beyond words. How could she sleep in here? But Pam turned slowly to look at it. "It's beautiful!" she cried. "Two shades of gorgeous purple! My very favorite!"

Kathleen laughed and nodded. "I decorated it special for you, Pammy. I knew you'd love it."

Pam flew into Kathleen's arms and hugged her hard. Terryl turned away, jealousy rising inside her. She thought she'd scream—or burst into wild tears, which would be worse.

"Which suitcases are yours, Terryl?" asked David, smiling down at her from his great height.

She hesitated, then pointed to her cases and watched in surprise as he picked them up and started for the door. She frowned, then looked helplessly at Mom.

Kathleen laughed at the look on Terryl's face, and reached out for her hand. "Wait'll you see your room, Terryl. You girls have always had to share a room, but now you each have your own. Isn't that wonderful?"

Pam spun around the purple room with her arms out and a wide smile on her face. A room of her very own! It was more than she'd ever dreamed possible.

Terryl walked across the hall with Mom, too stunned to object to anything. She followed David into the room, her insides churning. *If the room is purple*, she thought angrily, *I'll get sick all over the thick carpet!*

She stopped abruptly just inside the room and looked around first in surprise, then in awe and delight. Two years ago—before the divorce—she'd found a picture of a beautiful bedroom in a magazine. She'd showed it to Mom, then tacked it on her bulletin board, saying that some day she'd have a room just like it. And now, here it was! It was done in bright, cheerful shades of orange, green, and yellow. (Not a purple thread was in sight.) She walked across the plush carpet, blinking back the tears that threatened to fall. Was this a dream? Was this room really hers?

"I knew you'd like it," said Kathleen softly as she pulled Terryl close in her arms.

"I love it!" Terryl hugged Mom tightly just as Pam walked into the room.

Pam bit back a cry of disgust. How could Terryl like such ugly colors? Finally she shrugged. If Terryl liked it, then she'd try to keep from saying anything bad about it.

David stood beside the door, almost filling the room. He fingered his dark beard and studied the twins and Kathleen. Terryl looked up and her dark eyes locked with his. He smiled slowly and she ducked her head and pulled away from Mom.

"I'll unpack," Terryl said stiffly. "I brought a picture of Dad to put on the nightstand."

David didn't flicker an eyelash. He handed her a suitcase and she took it, making sure her hand didn't touch his. He winked at her and she frowned fiercely.

Kathleen slipped her hand through David's arm. "Let's leave the girls alone to settle in." She turned to the girls with a smile. "I'll be up later when Dani comes home."

The girls nodded without speaking. Terryl held her breath until the door closed after David and Mom, then let it out with an angry "I hate it here!" She flung herself down on her multicolored bedspread. "I hate *him!*"

Pam eased toward the door. "I'm going to unpack," she said as she opened it. She didn't want Terryl to force her to say she hated it here, too.

Terryl picked up the suitcase that held the photograph of Dad and pulled out the eight-by-ten picture of a man who looked deep in thought. She held the picture to her racing heart, waiting for it to soothe her.

Pam ran to her room and looked around with a smile spread across her face. She had Sugar and a purple bedroom—and David didn't seem so bad. He was nothing like Dad, but maybe she'd get used to him.

In her room Terryl slowly set the photograph on the stand beside the lamp with butterflies on it. "Dad, you should've let me stay with you," she whispered around the tight lump in her throat.

She sank to the carpet with her back pressed against the bed and stared at Dad's picture until the image of David's smile and wink faded away.

five
The Keyes Family

"I think it's awful that we can't have a room together, Pam." Terryl sat crossed-legged on Pam's bed and watched her put her jeans and underwear in the chest of drawers.

Pam slowly closed the drawer. "Yeah, awful," she said carefully. Really it was great to have things her own way instead of Terryl's way, but she didn't want to make Terryl mad by saying so.

"I bet you can't sleep all by yourself, Pam. You get scared alone at night. You get scared with me in a bed beside you." Terryl narrowed her dark eyes and studied Pam's back. It wasn't like Pam to treat her so casually. Pam always hung on her every word, and jumped at any suggestion that she made. Could it be possible that Pam was actually glad to be here, glad about Mom and David? "I know you'll be afraid to sleep in here alone," Terryl insisted.

Pam flushed and turned to face Terryl. "I don't think I'll be scared here. David is so big that no burglar would dare break in."

Terryl scrambled off the bed and walked around the room. The purple was really beginning to bother

her. She peeked into the hallway. The colors there were tans and browns with white. "I wonder what Dani's room looks like."

"We'll find out when she gets here."

"Let's go see now."

"Oh, Terryl!" Pam backed away, shaking her head.

"Oh, come on, Pam. We won't touch anything or steal anything. We'll just look." It suddenly seemed very important for Terryl to peek into Dani's room and she was determined that she would do it, no matter what Pam said. "Come on, Pam. Let's go look."

Pam sighed heavily as she followed Terryl down the hall to Dani's room. Music drifted up from downstairs, and smells of coffee and fried chicken hung on the air. Terryl sniffed appreciatively, then suddenly realized she was starving. *Dani's room first,* she thought, *then food.*

Pam hung back, glancing furtively around as Terryl opened Dani's door. Terryl peeked inside and finally her sister did too. The room was done in varying shades of pink with flowered wallpaper and curtains with matching bedspread. A big pink rag doll flopped against several flowered throw cushions resting against pink pillows.

"Dani must be a sissy little girl," whispered Terryl, wrinkling her small nose. "I'm not going to like her at all."

Pam nodded, but she thought maybe she'd like Dani if she wasn't a tomboy the way Terryl was. With a flush Pam pushed the thought aside. She loved Terryl just the way she was. Of course she did! If Terryl didn't want to like Dani, then maybe she wouldn't either. With trembling hands she tucked her hair behind her ears and followed Terryl to her room.

Several minutes later Kathleen knocked on Terryl's door, then pushed it open. "I heard you girls in here," she said breathlessly. "I brought Dani up."

Dani stepped into the room, her blue eyes wide with laughter. "Hi, girls! Who's Terryl and who's Pam? Dad said he didn't think I'd ever be able to tell you apart." Dani wore jeans and a light blue blouse with a dark blue sweater pulled over it. Her hair was a mass of blonde curls and her face was suntanned and beautiful. She was dainty and gorgeous and full of life.

Kathleen stood beside the twins. "Dani, this is Pam and this is Terryl. Not many people can tell them apart. Even I confuse them when they're trying to fool me."

"Hi," said Pam uncertainly, staring in surprise at Dani.

Terryl was speechless—Dani was not at all what she'd expected. She seemed very sure of herself, and very open and friendly. It would be hard to dislike her.

"There has to be a way to tell you apart." Dani cocked her head and studied them carefully, her blue eyes twinkling. "I'll figure it out." She looked up at Kathleen. "Why did you name the twins the way you did? I thought twins had names that sounded alike or started alike."

Kathleen sat on the edge of Terryl's bed and crossed her long legs. "It's a long story, Dani, but it all comes down to the fact that I named Pam and

Richard named Terryl. We both picked names that we liked."

"Is that Richard?" Dani pointed to the photograph on the nightstand.

"That's Dad," said Terryl firmly.

Dani stepped closer to the picture. "He's very good-looking. I checked his books out of the library and read them. They were good."

Terryl blinked in surprise. She had tried to read Dad's books, but they were too long and boring and she could never get past the first three pages.

Pam rubbed her hands up and down her arms, unable to believe that Dani would really read Dad's books, and then be able to talk about it as if he wasn't a complication in her life.

"I might be a writer someday," continued Dani. "I read a lot. But I want to be a rancher, too; I love horses and cattle. Do you girls want to see my horse?"

"Of course they do," said Kathleen brightly, too brightly it seemed to Terryl. "Take them to the barn and show them, but don't stay long. Diane has supper almost ready."

The twins shot a look at Kathleen and asked at the same time, "Who's Diane?"

"She's our housekeeper and cook," said Kathleen.

"She's been with us over a year already," said Dani. "She's a good cook. She makes great tacos. I'll introduce you to her on the way out." She walked to the door and turned with a smile. "Coming?"

"Of course they are." Kathleen gently nudged the twins toward the door. "Wear your jackets. It's a little too chilly to go outside without them."

Terryl grabbed her jacket as Pam ran across to her room for hers.

"Get acquainted with your new home, girls," said Kathleen.

Terryl wished she could refuse to go, but she knew Mom would insist, so she flipped back her honey-brown hair and walked down the hall with Pam and Dani.

In the kitchen Dani stopped the twins. "Diane, I want you to meet the Tyler twins."

Diane turned from the counter where she was chopping a salad. Her eyes widened and she laughed. "You really are identical, aren't you?" Diane was average size with streaked blonde hair cut short. She wore a flowered apron over faded jeans and a red blouse with sleeves rolled almost to her elbows. "Your mother has talked about you so much, I feel like I know you."

"This is Pam and this is Terryl." Dani felt proud of herself for being able to get the names right. She'd noticed the colors in their jackets. As long as they didn't change jackets, she could tell them apart. "We're going out to see the horses."

"Your grandparents should be riding in soon." Diane said as she reached for a carrot. She smiled at the twins. "Girls, I'm very glad to meet you. If you ever want anything special to eat, let me know and I'll do what I can to make it."

"Thanks," said Terryl in surprise. "Do you know how to make cream puffs?" She'd had cream puffs in the bakery with Dad several times and she'd always wanted to know how to make them.

Diane nodded. "I'll make them for you tomorrow."

"You will?" Terryl couldn't believe her ears. Mom had never been much of a cook and Dad didn't know how to make anything out of the ordinary. "Thanks!"

"What about you, Pam?" asked Diane with a wide smile.

Pam bit her bottom lip thoughtfully. "Chocolate mousse?" She'd had it last Sunday when Dad had taken them out for dinner.

Diane's dark eyebrows shot up. "Now, that's a little harder, but I'll sure try."

"Make me tacos," said Dani with a giggle.

"I know all about what you like, little miss." Diane tipped back her head and sang in a beautiful clear voice, "Well, Dani likes tacos, burritos, and chili. She eats chicken and steak with peas and broccoli." She kept on with the song until all three girls were laughing hard.

A few minutes later the girls walked into the late afternoon sunshine, still laughing. Terryl liked Diane and she knew Pam did too. Liking Diane wasn't being disloyal to her family, was it?

"There's my horse," said Dani, pointing to a pinto pony in the pen beside the longest barn. "Her name's Lizzy."

Lizzy lifted her head, then raced across the grassy field and slid to a stop at the wooden fence. She nickered, bobbing her head.

Dani ran to the fence and reached through to rub

Lizzy's face. "I brought my new sisters for you to meet. This is Pam and this is Terryl."

Pam slowly reached out and touched Lizzy. Terryl wanted to leap over the fence and try to ride the horse, but she held back. Being called Dani's sister had erased most of her excitement about seeing Lizzy.

"Look! Here come Gran and Grandad!" Dani pointed and the twins looked up to see two people on horseback riding toward them.

Terryl sagged against the fence and stared. Grandmother would never in all her life ride a horse, nor dress in jeans!

Pam looked, blinked her eyes, and looked again. "Are you teasing us, Dani? That's not really your gran and grandad, is it?"

Dani frowned. "Why do you say that?"

"Grandparents don't ride horses or wear cowboy hats."

"Mine do." Dani laughed. "Gran says she would never sit around in the house and knit or go to teas or even cook dinner. She has always worked outdoors and she loves it. She trains the horses and buys new ones. Grandad is in charge of the cattle. Today they were checking fences."

"What does your dad do? Nothing?" Terryl grinned and shot a look at Pam.

Pam watched for some reaction from Dani, but she only smiled.

"Dad works hard at everything. He finds buyers for the horses and cattle, he keeps the books, and he does regular work around the ranch." Dani walked toward the gate to open it for her grandparents, and the twins trailed behind her.

They watched as the two people dismounted. Gran took off her hat, showing white hair pressed to her head. Her blue eyes sparkled and she smiled. She was short, slight, and wiry, and her skin looked like old leather. With a happy shout she hugged first Terryl, then Pam.

"I'm so glad to meet you beautiful youngsters," she said in a voice that to Terryl seemed too loud in such a small person. "Grandad, don't these girls just beat all?"

He took off his hat and rubbed his hand across his bald head, his blue eyes twinkling as he laughed. "You girls are as alike as two peas in a pod. But I'd swear you're the prettiest peas in this world, right along with Dani-girl." Grandad was tall and thin and dressed in jeans, boots, and a jacket that matched his jeans. His voice cracked when he talked as if he'd overused it in the past.

Terryl wanted to turn and run away from them before she grew to like them the way she had Diane, but she couldn't move away from the looks of delight that they were giving her and Pam. They really seemed to be glad they were on the Big Key. Terryl couldn't understand how anyone could be so nice.

Pam looked from Gran to Grandad. "We're glad to meet you both, too. I think we're going to have fun here."

Terryl stared in shock at Pam—Pam never spoke up first! She narrowed her eyes and tried to think of a way to force Pam back into the role of the twin who always stayed in the background. But she couldn't think of anything, and finally gave it up to listen to Gran talk about the new foal that had just been born.

"Come to the barn and I'll show you girls," said Gran, clamping her hat on her head.

Terryl walked with the others, too anxious to see the baby horse to think about what she should or shouldn't do to keep from enjoying her stay at the Big Key Ranch.

six
The Birthday Party

"We'd better hustle to the house for supper," Gran said as she locked the stall door. The foal whinnied and the girls laughed. "We don't want to miss Diane's delicious fried chicken."

Terryl hung back for one last look at the brown foal, then ran to catch up with the others as they walked out of the barn. The dogs met them and, to her surprise, Malcom chose to walk beside her. She walked with her hand on his head.

"He sure did take to you," said Grandad, shaking his head. "Last month when your mother bought him he wouldn't have anything to do with any of us at first. Finally he made friends, but it took him a while. But not with you, Terryl. You got yourself a fine dog."

Terryl puffed out with pride. "I always wanted a dog."

Grandad chuckled. "It seems Malcom always wanted a Terryl."

She ducked her head to hide a pleased smile and she gave Malcom one last pat before she followed the others into the house. Smells of supper made her stomach rumble hungrily.

Kathleen poked her head out of the dining room. "Girls, wash quickly. We don't want Diane's supper to spoil."

Pam could tell by Mom's face that she was very excited about something. With a smile Pam ran upstairs with Dani and Terryl right behind her. Maybe Mom asked Diane to bake them a birthday cake. Maybe they'd even get presents. Then Pam shook her head as she stepped into her bathroom to wash; Sugar was the only gift she wanted.

In her room Terryl washed and brushed her hair, then ran to look out the window to see if she could get another glimpse of Malcom before she went to eat. She saw the empty side yard and an open field, but no Malcom. With a sigh she turned around and saw the photograph of Dad. For a while she'd forgotten about him and her plan to hate it here.

"I won't forget again," she whispered grimly. "I'll go to supper, but I won't talk to anyone and I won't eat much." Her stomach growled. Well, maybe she'd eat enough so that she wasn't hungry, but she wouldn't enjoy any of it.

With short jerky movements she pushed her clean tee shirt into her jeans and walked to Pam's room. Pam had better not let herself have fun now or any of the time that they were here on the Big Key!

"Hurry, girls," called Dani, her eyes sparkling with excitement. "We have to get to supper right now!"

"I'm ready," said Pam, deliberately not looking at Terryl. She knew Terryl would ruin the rest of the day if she could and she wasn't going to give her a chance. Pam lifted her chin higher as she walked beside Dani down the stairs. For the first time ever she felt like a whole person. She had a room of her own in a color that she loved, and she had a dog of her own. If she didn't want to share with Terryl, she didn't have to. If she didn't want to do what Terryl wanted, she didn't have to. It was a whole new feeling and she wanted to hang onto it as long as possible.

Dani stopped Pam outside the dining room door and waited for Terryl. "I want us to walk in together."

Pam shrugged. "All right."

Terryl stopped beside Pam, her brows cocked questioningly.

"Let's go in, shall we?" Dani nudged the twins and they walked into the dining room.

"Surprise! Happy birthday, girls!"

Pam's eyes widened as she looked at the decorations around the room. Balloons of all colors and sizes practically filled the room. A gigantic birthday cake stood on a table, candles flickering. Gaily wrapped packages covered another table. Helplessly Pam looked at Terryl, but she was too surprised and overcome to notice.

Kathleen kissed Terryl, then Pam. "Make wishes and blow out the candles, girls. After that we'll eat and you can open gifts."

Terryl walked slowly to the cake decorated in yellow and green and white. She saw the words "Happy Birthday Pam and Terryl" written across the top. Tears stung her eyes and she blinked them away as she took a deep breath. Together she and Pam blew out the twenty candles, ten for her and ten for Pam. The others in the room clapped and shouted and it was different than anything she'd ever experienced before. She could tell Pam was just as overwhelmed. The party they'd had at lunch with Dad had been nice, but it'd been quiet and very proper without any shouting or laughing or clapping.

Finally they all sat at the table that was also decorated with flowers and name cards. Terryl, Pam, and Dani sat on one side of the table, Gran, Grandad, and a man they hadn't met before sat across from them. David sat at the head of the table with Kathleen at the other end. The dining room seemed larger than Dad's entire apartment.

Suddenly everyone grew very quiet. The twins looked at Mom questioningly and she smiled then bowed her head. Terryl swallowed hard and did the same thing. Pam locked her hands together in her lap and stared at her fancy china plate.

"Heavenly Father," prayed David. "We thank you for this wonderful day and for the special girls with us. Bless both Pam and Terryl on this birthday and help them to have the very best year they've ever had. Thank you for this food. In Jesus' name, amen."

A tingle went through Pam and she looked at David. He smiled at her and she smiled back before she remembered that Terryl was probably watching and would be angry.

Terryl fingered her napkin, unsure how she really felt about David's prayer. It was strange to pray over a meal, and stranger still to have someone pray for her and Pam.

"Girls, I want you to meet David's younger

brother, Mark," said Kathleen, indicating the man beside Gran. "He wanted to be here for your party. Mark, this is Pam and Terryl."

"I'm very glad to meet you both," said Mark in a voice that sounded much like David's. Mark was tall and lean with dark hair and blue eyes. He wore dress pants and a white shirt and gray sweater. "Welcome to this wild family. Terryl, I hear you play violin."

She nodded, surprised that he knew and that Mom would even mention it since she didn't care much for music lessons.

"Mark plays too," said Gran, patting his muscular arm. "He started when he was nine. We're very proud of him."

"He'll play for you later," said Grandad with a nod. "We never let him visit us without hearing a song or two." Grandad turned to smile at David as he reached for a bowl of mashed potatoes. "Now, David here can't play anything but the radio. Unless of course it's the TV." Everyone but Terryl laughed.

She forked a piece of crispy fried chicken onto her plate and concentrated on passing the food after she helped herself to a little of each. To keep from talking, she ate the broccoli with cheese sauce, mashed potatoes, tossed salad with Marie's Ranch Dressing, fried chicken, and fresh baked rolls with melted butter. Before she realized what was happening she was enjoying every morsel. The teasing and laughing at the meal were something new to her, and she caught herself listening and even laughing.

Pam relaxed for the first time that she could

remember at a meal. With Dad she was always afraid she'd say something that he'd think was dumb. And with Mom alone she'd always been afraid that she'd say something about Dad that would hurt her. Even with Terryl Pam felt as if she had to guard every word, every expression on her face. But tonight there were so many people that she could enjoy her meal and listen to the others. Eight people at a meal were more fun than just three.

David pushed back his chair. "Time to open the gifts now. Diane will clear the table so that we can have cake and ice cream afterward."

Kathleen slipped her hand through David's strong arm and smiled at the twins. "The gifts on the left side of the table are yours, Terryl, and the ones on the right are yours, Pam."

They had never received so many gifts on their birthday. But then, they'd never had such a large family before to share their birthday with, either.

Dani stood at the side of the table, barely able to stand still. "Open mine first! Please, please!" She pointed to a yellow and pink box and Pam picked it up and started to tear off the paper. Dani showed Terryl a red and blue box and Terryl picked it up to open it.

Both girls opened their boxes at the same time and lifted out baseball mitts. Terryl slipped hers on and held it up as Pam did the same.

"We were going to join the softball team," Pam said. "But we couldn't. We almost bought mitts, but all Terryl got were the caps."

Terryl dropped the mitt as everyone talked about playing ball and how all the kids in the neighborhood got together to play. She looked at the other gifts and finally pulled a large box to her and lifted the lid. Her eyes widened. Inside was a fancy pair of western boots that she'd always dreamed about having someday. She read the card to find that Gran and Grandad had bought them for her. She smiled her thanks and they nodded and beamed as if she'd given them a gift.

By the time they finished opening gifts, they had jeans and shirts and things for their rooms. Terryl received a wooden music stand from Uncle Mark and Pam laughed in delight at the framed picture of Sugar to hang in her room.

"Thank you, thank you, everybody!" cried Pam with an excitement that she very seldom expressed.

"Yeah, thanks," said Terryl just above a whisper.

"You're very welcome," said David with a wink and smile. Then Dani pushed back her chair.

"Terryl and Pam," she said smiling, "it's time for the rest of your surprise."

The twins looked at Kathleen. She nodded and smiled, and finally they followed Dani out to the hallway. Dani held out their jackets to them, then slipped her own on. "We have to go outdoors for this."

Bursting with curiosity the girls followed Dani to the backyard. The sun was down, but the yard was lit with lights much like street lights. Suddenly children of all sizes leaped from behind bushes and yelled, "Happy birthday!"

Terryl and Pam stood side by side and looked at the boys and girls standing in a cluster. "Thank you," they said together in small voices.

"They came to play," said Dani. "They can stay until 8:30. We'll play tag first."

"I don't want to play tag," said a tall dark-haired girl as she crossed her arms over her chest.

"Don't make trouble, Sarah James," snapped Dani. "This is a party, and you aren't going to fight with anyone or I'll make you go home."

"Oh, yeah?" Sarah stepped close to Dani, towering over her. "You're such a shrimp that you couldn't do anything."

Terryl and Pam walked to Dani's side. "With our help, she can," stated Terryl.

Dani grinned at the twins. "Thanks, but Sarah won't make trouble. Will you, Sarah?"

Sarah wrinkled her nose and shrugged.

Dani quickly introduced all the neighborhood children to the twins and the game of tag began. Soon shouts and laughter filled the yard on the cool September evening.

Several minutes later Pam bumped into Terryl, and laughed. "This is sure fun, isn't it?"

Terryl started to agree, then stopped herself. "I guess if you like little kid stuff." She saw the sparkle leave Pam's face and she turned away with a satisfied, smug look. She'd just have to keep reminding Pam that they were here to try to make Mom give up her life with David and go back to Dad.

Then a great sadness settled over Terryl and she ducked behind a bush to be alone. Would it really be better for everyone if Mom and Dad were back together? Mom seemed so happy now, and so did Dad. Oh, why did their lives have to be so complicated?

SEVEN
A Talk with Mom

Terryl slumped against a tree, panting for breath after a wild game of soccer. She had wanted to hang back and not join in with all the neighborhood kids, but they had urged her into the games and finally she'd given up her desire to show everyone that she was angry that she was away from Dad on her birthday. She'd started having too much fun to think about Dad, or the divorce, or Mom's new husband.

Just then the back door opened and Kathleen walked out with a jacket over her slender shoulders. "Time to come in for cake and ice cream, kids."

Shouts of delight rose up around Terryl and Pam and they laughed, then ran with everyone into the house to the dining room where plates were already set for all of them. Mark stood to the side of the table with his violin in his hand. He smiled at Terryl and she smiled back.

"Your violin is beautiful," she said as she gingerly stroked the shiny wood. "Are you going to play now?"

Mark nodded. "I thought this would be a good time. It'll keep the roar of this crowd down enough so that the others in the house can think." He grinned and tapped Terryl's shoulder with the bow. "Take your place and the music will begin."

A warm feeling spread inside Terryl and she sat down to enjoy cake and ice cream with the others. The table looked even bigger now with everyone seated around it.

David waited for everyone to settle down, then turned to Diane. "Serve the birthday girls first, please."

Diane nodded as she sliced the bottom layer of the chocolate cake while everyone sat gazing hungrily at the dishes of vanilla ice cream in front of them.

Terryl had never tasted such delicious chocolate cake. She opened her mouth to tell Diane how good it was just as Pam did. Terryl stared at Pam in surprise. Was this really the same twin that was always so quiet, so afraid of everything? A spark of respect for Pam grew inside Terryl, surprising her even more. She had always loved Pam because she was her sister, but she'd often thought she was too quiet. Suddenly Pam was different, and Terryl knew it would take her a while to get used to it.

While they ate Mark played his violin, going from one lilting melody to another. Terryl's fingers itched to get her violin and join in with Mark, but she knew she needed more practice before she was as good as he was. Someday, though, she would be! Someday he'd tell her that she could easily play professionally and she would smile and nod and agree with him.

Pam ate her vanilla ice cream, slowly listening

with half an ear to the music. She liked music, but it didn't mean as much to her as it did to Terryl. Pam knew she'd never waste her valuable time practicing hour after hour. She'd rather spend her time with Sugar, training him to obey and teaching him tricks. Tomorrow she'd start to teach him to shake hands and fetch.

Just then Sarah James pushed back her chair and stood up. "I don't want to hear any more of that dumb music. I'm going home."

Before anyone could say anything, she marched out of the room. Terryl wanted to run after her and drag her back to apologize to Mark, but she didn't move. She glanced toward Mark, but he was still smiling as if Sarah's rude outburst hadn't bothered him at all.

Several minutes later everyone said good night and ran home. Mark locked his violin in the case.

"I'd better get home too," he said. "Happy birthday again, girls. I'll be seeing you soon. I spend a lot of time here just to get away from my lonely apartment in Grand Rapids."

"You play beautifully." Terryl looked up at him, her cheeks flushed brightly. "Some day I want to play as well as you do."

"Thanks. Next time I come I want you to play for me." He squeezed her shoulder and smiled.

She nodded happily, and asked, "Will you be here tomorrow?"

"Not tomorrow, but maybe Sunday." He told her good night again, then walked out to find the others to say good-bye.

Terryl looked after him for a few minutes, then

suddenly realized that Dani and Pam were stacking the dishes. She turned to help them.

"You girls don't have to do this since it's your birthday," said Dani.

"We don't mind," said Pam with a load of plates in her hands.

"I thought Diane did this," said Terryl.

"She does," Dani answered, reaching for a fork. "But I always help clear off the table. I like to help her."

Terryl reached for the drinking glasses just as Diane walked in. Diane stopped in surprise.

"Girls, thank you! I needed your help for this, and I appreciate it. I'm not as young as I used to be and I have a tendency to get tired this time of night." She tipped back her head and laughed. "Did I just say that? You'd think I was getting old or something." She set a tray on the table and began to fill it with dishes and silverware. "It might be fun to be ten again." She grinned at the girls. "I don't quite remember when I was ten . . . let me see, Was it fifteen years ago, or twenty five? Did I live at home yet, or was I already a housekeeper somewhere?"

Dani giggled. "Were you a housekeeper when you were ten?"

Diane frowned thoughtfully. "No. I started when I was eight, I think. Or was it six? You see, I was always very grown up for my age. Why, I bet when I was ten I was really twenty."

Terryl and Pam saw the twinkle in Diane's eyes and knew she was joking with them. They had never met anyone quite like Diane before. She was a fun person to be around.

A few minutes later the dining room was clear and Diane had the dishwasher in the kitchen filled and working. Kathleen poked her head in the doorway.

"Time for bed, girls. Thank you for helping Diane." Kathleen turned to Diane. "Thank you for the wonderful birthday dinner and cake. You made this day very special."

Terryl stared in surprise at her mom. She'd never told the cleaning lady who used to come to their apartment thank you, or said that she'd done a good job.

"I was glad to do it," said Diane. She leaned down and kissed each of the girls on the cheek. "Sleep tight, girls. See you at breakfast."

"How about pancakes for breakfast?" asked Dani.

"I can manage that."

"And chocolate mousse," said Pam with a giggle.

Diane shrugged, smiling. "If you can eat it, I can fix it." Then she laughed. "No, not for breakfast, but I'll make it for supper. Is that all right?"

"Will you teach me how to make it? I want to learn so I can make some when we live with Dad." The sparkle left Pam's eyes and she ducked her head. After today she didn't know if she could live with Dad again. Guilt rose inside her and almost choked her. Of course she could live with Dad again. She loved him, didn't she? Sure she did!

"I'll teach you how," said Diane softly. "See you in the morning."

Kathleen herded the girls upstairs and instructed them to take showers and dress in warm night-gowns. "I'll be in to tuck you in later."

Much later Terryl slipped between the sheets of her bed and lay with her eyes wide open and her light still on. Her head spun with the activity of the day. With a tired sigh she turned her head until she could see Dad's picture. "Pam wants to learn how to make chocolate mousse for you. Isn't that dumb? She didn't even remember that you don't like it. I would've reminded her, but I didn't want to make her feel bad in front of the others."

Terryl sighed again. She really hadn't said anything because she'd been afraid that she'd burst into tears. The day had been wonderful even without Dad and she hated herself for feeling that way. At least she had managed to stay away from David. Mark didn't count; he hadn't married Mom.

Kathleen knocked and walked in, tying her rosy pink bathrobe around her narrow waist. She sat on the edge of the bed and smoothed Terryl's hair back from her face. "I'm so glad to have you here, honey. I want to make the most of our nine months together. I've even found a violin teacher for you with Mark's help. Mark says he's first rate."

"I . . . I didn't think you wanted me to take lessons."

"Terryl, I've learned a lot since I asked Jesus to be Lord of my life. I know how to put others before myself now. Since playing violin is important to you, then it's important to me too. I want you to become the best Terryl Tyler possible. You don't have to be like Pam or like me or even like Dad. You can be yourself."

Terryl thought about that for a while and didn't know what to say. "Mom, can't you learn to love

Dad again so we can all be a happy family the way we used to be?"

Kathleen picked up Terryl's hand and held it. "Terryl, we were never a happy family. You couldn't see that because you were too young and then when you were older your dad and I both hid our true feelings. It was hard on me when Dad said he wanted a divorce, but in the end it was the best thing for both of us."

"No!" Terryl's voice was choked with tears.

"Divorce is a terrible thing, honey," Kathleen said gently, "and I'm sorry it happened. But it did happen, and we have to go on living. If we'd been a Christian family, we'd have been able to ask the Lord to help us build a life together, but we weren't. We didn't know what to do to keep our marriage together, so we had to move apart. I'm sorry about it, but that's the way it is." She kissed Terryl's warm cheek.

"Now I'm married to David and we are a Christian family. I'm sure you have felt the happiness and joy and heard the laughter in this family. It's because of God. He is our heavenly Father and the head of this family, and he always will be."

"Doesn't Dad like God?"

"He doesn't know him, Terryl. I'm praying that someone will tell him about God so that he can know him." Kathleen kissed Terryl again. "Close your eyes and go to sleep now. God is with you and will help you to sleep well. He loves you, Terryl."

"But he doesn't know me!"

Kathleen smiled tenderly. "Oh, he knows you. And

I hope that soon you'll know him." She stood up and clicked off the lamp. "See you in the morning."

Terryl curled on her side and snuggled against her pillow. Did God really love her? He must or Mom wouldn't have said it. She thought about that as she drifted off to sleep.

In Pam's room, Kathleen talked to Pam about the same thing, and she nodded. "You know, Mom, I've prayed to God a few times. But I didn't really know how, so I quit."

"Praying is just talking to God or to Jesus, Pam. It's not hard at all." Kathleen told Pam that God wanted to be her heavenly Father and that Jesus wanted to be her Savior and Lord and friend. "While you're here, Pam, I'll help you to get to know God personally. Would you like that?"

"Yes," whispered Pam.

Kathleen kissed Pam's flushed cheek. "I want this to be the best nine months you've ever had. I love you very much."

"Mom, can't we ever live together again?"

"No, honey, we can't. Our lives are fixed this way and we have to make the most of it. I wish it could be different, but it isn't." Kathleen hugged Pam close. "We can learn to live with being different, can't we?"

Pam thought about that for a while. "I guess so." She knew she could try, but she was afraid that Terryl wouldn't. Terryl could make things really hard when she wanted to. "I love you, Mom."

"And I love you, Pam. You're a precious little girl."

Pam smiled as she watched Mom click off the

lamp and walk out. With a contented sigh Pam
pulled the covers to her chin and closed her eyes.

Kathleen walked to Dani's room and Dani looked
up with a glad smile.

"I thought you might forget me since your own
girls are here," said Dani just above a whisper, as
Kathleen came to sit on the edge of her bed.

"I would never forget you, Dani. You're my
daughter, too, and I love you very much." She kissed
her good night.

"I love you, Kathleen."

"Thank you, Dani."

"I might be able to call you Mom one of these
days since Terryl and Pam do."

"Whenever you're ready, Dani. Good night."

Dani closed her eyes and listened as Kathleen
walked out into the hallway. A tear slipped from the
corner of her eye and she wiped it away.

EIGHT
Sarah James

Saturday afternoon Terryl looked up from playing
with Malcom to see the girl from across the road
riding her bike down the driveway. Terryl frowned.
She remembered the girl was Sarah James, the rude
girl with the big nose.

Dani ran to stand beside Terryl. "Oh, no, it's Sarah
James. I told her she couldn't come over today."

"Hi, Dani," called Sarah. "Hi, whichever twin you
are." Sarah wore faded jeans and a red sweatshirt
without a jacket. The sun turned her black hair
almost blue. "Lock your dogs up so I can play."

"You go home and they won't bother you." Dani
held Lassie's collar to keep her from running to sniff
Sarah.

"I won't go home." Sarah dropped her bike in the
grass. "I came to play." She stood with her fists on
her hips and her chin thrust out. "The Peters kids
went to town with their mom, so I have to play with
you girls."

Terryl stood with her arms over Malcom's back.
"Who says you have to?"

Sarah frowned at her. "Who are you anyway?"

"She's Terryl," said Dani, pleased with herself for knowing. It was all because of Malcom. If Pam wasn't still inside, and if Terryl hadn't walked right to Malcom when they came out, then Dani wouldn't have known which twin was with her.

Sarah shook her finger at Terryl. "Well, Terryl, you better listen to me. I play where I want to play and right now I want to play here."

"You're a big bully!" Terryl tugged on Malcom's collar. "We won't play with you. So there!"

"You just think you're hot stuff because you had a birthday yesterday and got all those presents and had that big party. My birthday is going to be in three months and I'll be eleven years old and I'm going to get more gifts than you did and have a bigger party."

Dani shook her head. "You never have a party, Sarah. Your parents are always too busy working to remember your birthday."

Terryl saw pain flash in Sarah's eyes.

Sarah tugged down her sweatshirt. "At least I have two parents! My mother didn't die like yours did, Dani. And my parents aren't divorced like yours are, Terryl. Terrible Terryl!"

Dani blinked back tears. "I'll never play with you, Sarah James! Do you hear me? I never will!"

Sarah chuckled smugly. "Want to bet? Your new mom'll make you. She thinks we're good friends." Sarah looked around. "Where is Mrs. Keyes? Is she working in the greenhouse again?"

"She's not in the greenhouse," snapped Dani.

Terryl stepped toward Sarah and Malcom walked

with her. "You don't need to know where Mom is. You go home right now!"

Sarah looked uneasily at Malcom, then looked defiantly at Terryl. "I will not go home! You can't make me!"

Terryl stepped closer, and so did Malcom. "I might be littler than you, but I'm strong!"

Sarah stared at Malcom and sucked in her breath. Terryl saw Sarah's fear and took one more step forward. Sarah fell back two steps, her blue eyes wide and her round cheeks pale.

Terryl crossed her thin arms over her thin chest. "If you don't leave right now we'll turn the dogs loose on you."

"Oh, Terryl," whispered Dani, gripping Lassie's collar tighter.

Sarah looked uncertainly from Dani to Terryl and to the dogs beside them. "You wouldn't do that." She didn't sound sure of herself and Terryl grinned.

"Dani might not since she's a Christian, but I would." She pushed Malcom forward. "Go get her, Malcom!"

Sarah ran screaming toward the house with Terryl after her, shouting for Malcom to bite Sarah. Dani caught at Terryl's arm.

"Stop it, Terryl. You'll get in a lot of trouble if you don't stop right now!" Dani grabbed Terryl's arm with both hands and Lassie suddenly realized she was free. She barked and ran after Sarah, too, blocking her way with a snarl.

With a bloodcurdling cry Sarah whipped around only to bump into Malcom. She tumbled to the grass, sobbing. "Don't let him bite me," she whimpered, cringing in fear.

Just then Kathleen ran out the door, a concerned look on her face. "What is going on out here? Sarah, did the dogs hurt you?"

Sarah scrambled to her feet, her eyes flashing. She pointed at Dani and Terryl who huddled together. "They did it! They made the dogs attack me! I didn't do nothing. I came to play and be nice, but they hate me and they sicced the dogs on me so I'd have to go home."

Kathleen frowned at the girls before she turned back to Sarah to brush her off and see that she wasn't badly hurt. "Sarah, I'm sure the girls would be happy to play with you."

"We would not!" Terryl lifted her chin and her eyes flashed. "We don't want her here at all. She's mean."

Sarah ducked her head and tried to look very innocent. "I wouldn't be mean, Mrs. Keyes. I only want to play with them. I'm home all alone today and don't have nothing to do, so I came to play."

Kathleen walked around Sarah and stopped directly in front of Terryl. "I don't know what your father let you get away with, but here you can't be rude or mean. Do you understand? You will play with Sarah."

Terryl stared down at the grass and pressed her lips tightly together. How could Mom be so mean to her?

Kathleen turned to Dani. "As for you, young lady, you know better than to turn the dogs loose on Sarah. How could you do such a terrible thing? You and Sarah are friends. I want you to play together nicely with no more fighting or quarreling. Understand?"

Dani's eyes filled with tears and she nodded. She never wanted to play with Sarah again, but she knew she shouldn't argue with Kathleen. Dad had told her not to, and she wouldn't if she could help herself.

Terryl clenched her fists. "Mom, Dani didn't do anything! It was me. But mostly it was Sarah. She's not nice like she wants you to think she is."

"I am too!" cried Sarah.

Kathleen stood with her hands on her narrow waist and her head cocked. "Terryl, I don't want any argument."

Terryl stamped her small foot. "I don't care what you say, I will not play with Sarah and neither will Dani!"

"What's going on here?" David came up beside Kathleen and looked at the group. He narrowed his blue eyes thoughtfully as he looped his thumbs in his front jeans pockets. "I could hear you all the way to the barn."

Terryl locked her icy hands behind her back and pressed her lips tightly together. Didn't David know this wasn't his business?

Dani gulped as she moved closer to Lassie. "We don't want to play with Sarah," Dani said in a small voice.

"You don't, huh? Why is that?"

"It doesn't matter," said Kathleen firmly. "I told them they *will* play with Sarah, and that they will be nice to her."

"They sicced the dogs on me," piped up Sarah.

"What?" David frowned at Dani, then Terryl.

"It's true," said Sarah with a smug look on her round face.

Terryl moved restlessly, waiting for Dani to deny it, but Dani stood silently with her head down. "It is not true!" cried Terryl. "Dani didn't do anything. It was me. I told Malcom to bite Sarah so she'd leave us alone. But Malcom doesn't bite."

David nodded. "No, Malcom doesn't bite and he wouldn't know a command like that. But that doesn't mean you're without fault, Terryl. You can't give Malcom orders like that, nor can you ever use him to frighten others, or I'll take him away from you."

Terryl's eyes grew big and round and a band tightened around her heart. She tried to speak, but no sound slipped past the lump in her throat.

"Oh, David," whispered Kathleen.

David gripped Kathleen's arm. "Let's go inside and let the girls play. You hear that, girls? Play, not fight." He turned Kathleen toward the house and Terryl seethed inside as she watched them walk to the door.

Sarah grinned and pranced around. "See? Didn't I tell you? You have to play with me."

Anger rushed through Terryl and she thought her head would swell up and burst into a million pieces. "I don't care what anyone says, I will not play with you, Sarah James. I wouldn't play with you if you were the only girl in the whole wide world!"

Sarah stumbled back, a confused look on her face. "But they said you have to."

"Too bad! I won't do it and that's final!"

"What about you, Dani Keyes? You know you have to obey your dad."

Dani nodded her curly blonde head. "I have to obey him, but I don't have to like it. What do you want to play?"

Terryl gasped as she stared in disbelief at Dani. "Why should you have to obey him, Dani?"

"Because Jesus wants me to, Terryl." Dani smiled. "It's all right. Really. I'd rather obey and feel good inside, than disobey and be sorry later. Come on, Sarah. We'll swing together."

Terryl watched them run to the swing, then slowly turned and walked Malcom around the house. Being a Christian was sure strange.

NiNE
Sunday Surprises

Pam shook her head and backed away from Terryl until she bumped against her bed. "I don't want to wear my red suit, Terryl! I want to wear the new dress Mom bought for me. She bought it special for our first time of going to church with her."

Terryl flung Pam's red suit onto the bed, then doubled her fists at her sides. "You'd better wear it, Pam! We are going to look alike today so that no one can tell us apart!" Terryl didn't know exactly why it was so important that they wear the red suits that Dad had bought for them before they left Detroit, but she knew it was and she knew that Pam must do as she said. "If you don't wear it, Pam, I'll stay home today. And what would you do without me? You are scared to go to new places without me and you know it." Anger, frustration, and fear churned inside Terryl and she stepped right up to Pam, nose to nose. "You put on that red suit right now, Pam. I mean it!"

The color drained from Pam's face and she slowly turned and picked up the red suit. When Terryl acted like this, she couldn't stand up to her and fight for her own way. With trembling hands Pam dressed in the red suit. Tears threatened to fall, but she forced them back. Tears would only make things worse. She slipped on the shoes that hurt her feet and then stood beside Terryl, looking like the carbon copy that Terryl wanted.

"You have to take off the ring Dad gave you, Pam." Terryl pointed to Pam's right hand. "It's the only different thing about us."

Pam covered the ring with her hand and shook her head. She loved the ring and didn't want to leave it home. Finally she pulled it off and laid it on the dresser next to her hair brush. She wanted to scream and yell at Terryl, and tell her to stop being so mean, but she faced her silently.

Kathleen knocked and poked her head in. Then she shot into the room and stopped in front of the twins. "What are you girls doing? You had dresses to wear that I bought you. Why are you dressed alike?"

Terryl shrugged, but wouldn't speak. As long as she kept quiet and didn't take the lead, Mom wouldn't know if she was Pam or Terryl.

Pam shot a look at Terryl. "She said she wanted us to look alike today. She doesn't want anyone to be able to tell us apart."

Kathleen sighed heavily. "Oh, girls! Well, it's too late to change now. David and Dani are waiting downstairs for us. Come on." Kathleen held the door wide for them and they slowly walked into the quiet hallway. Kathleen wore an off-white linen suit with a blue silk blouse. Several gold chains hung down on her breast. She smelled like spring flowers. At the top of the stairs she stopped the twins. "Girls, you don't have to be afraid of this new experience.

78

Going to Sunday school and church is enjoyable. You'll see. Relax and have fun. Some of the kids that were at your birthday party will be there. And Dani will be with you." Kathleen smiled. "This is a very special day for me with you girls here!" She laughed softly. "Let's get going before we're late."

Terryl hung back, but Pam ran lightly down the stairs. Pam was suddenly eager for Sunday school and church. She and Mom had talked a lot about Jesus and Pam felt she was ready to open her heart to him.

With a thoughtful frown Terryl followed Pam. Being a Christian had made Mom very happy. It made Dani willing to obey her dad even when she didn't want to. It made the entire Keyes family full of love and care. Maybe being a Christian wasn't so bad. Maybe she'd become one after she had a chance to talk to Dad to see what he thought about it.

Dani ran to the twins with sparkling eyes. "I really can't tell you apart! This is fun! I think you are Pam and you are Terryl!" Dani laughed. "Am I right?"

"You're right," said Terryl even though Dani was wrong.

David laughed and fingered his beard. "No. I think you're teasing. I think you are Terryl. And I think you are Pam."

Kathleen slipped her hand through David's arm with a tinkling laugh. "You are correct, David. But how could you tell?"

Terryl scowled, wondering the same thing.

David grinned and shrugged. "I have my way, but I'll never tell." He ushered them outdoors to the car while everyone tried to guess how David told the twins apart.

Terryl sat in the seat directly behind David with Dani beside her and Pam on the other side of Dani. Gran and Grandad drove their own car to church. Diane had a day off, so the ranch seemed empty as David drove out of the yard. A bright sun turned the grass greener. Birds sang happily and the horses walked lazily around their pasture. Terryl wanted to jump from the car and run back to join the animals. She'd turn Malcom out of his kennel and they'd play the morning away while the others went to church.

Several minutes later Dani led the twins into the Sunday school wing of the huge church. Terryl wanted to turn and run, but Pam looked around eagerly, taking in the many rooms filled with boys and girls of all ages. They could hear laughter and singing and talking drifting through all the rooms.

Suddenly Sarah James blocked the doorway to the class. She frowned and shook her finger at the girls. "You don't belong here! I won't let you in!" Sarah looked plump and hot in her silky pink dress with ruffles and frills. Her little flowered bonnet had slipped sideways on her head and was perched over her right ear. Grass stains covered the toes of her white shoes. "Your clothes are too ugly."

"Stop it, Sarah," said Dani, stepping right up to her. Sarah stood almost a head taller than Dani and weighed several pounds more. "Move aside and let us in right now."

Terryl reached around Dani and pinched Sarah's arm just above her elbow.

Sarah squealed and jumped back. "You pinched me, whatever twin you are! You hurt me bad! You could've torn my new dress, you know!"

Terryl grinned and shrugged, then walked with Pam and Dani to empty seats at a long table. Several girls spoke to Dani, and she introduced them to the twins. Terryl was glad no one would be able to tell them apart.

Pam listened intently as the teacher talked about Jesus, but Terryl's mind wandered from Dad to the ranch to what she'd do to Sarah James once they were away from church.

After Sunday school Dani hurried them into the main part of the church to sit with David and Kathleen. Terryl moved restlessly, but she enjoyed the singing and was delightfully surprised to hear the man at the pulpit introduce a special guest to play the violin. She leaned forward and watched Mark walk to the front with his violin. He looked very handsome in his three piece navy blue suit and spotless white shirt. He smiled at the congregation and Terryl was sure his smile widened when he spotted her.

With a flourish he tucked the violin firmly under his chin, set the fingers of his left hand along the strings, and raised the bow. A hush fell and then the beautiful tones of the violin filled the sanctuary. The beauty of the music engulfed Terryl and almost took her breath away. Every fiber of her being was aware of the music and her hands itched to hold her violin and play in such a manner.

Applause rang out as Mark bowed and then

81

walked from the platform down the aisle. He stopped at the pew where Terryl sat and smiled down at her. She moved so he could sit beside her, and she realized she was glad that she'd come today. She would have hated to miss Mark's music.

After church, people swarmed around Mark, and Terryl was forced to back away from him and walk out with Pam and the others.

Outdoors Terryl spotted Sarah through the crowd, but her mind was so full of thoughts about violin music that she forgot about her plans for Sarah James.

"We have reservations at the Grand Plaza for dinner," said David as he opened the car doors. "Is anyone hungry?"

"I am," said Kathleen.

Terryl looked back at the crowd standing outside the church for signs of Mark, but couldn't see him. With a sigh she slipped into the back seat with Dani and Pam who were talking about what they were going to order for dinner.

David pulled out of the parking lot and eased onto the street. A pickup honked and children shouted. A warm breeze blew in through David's open window.

Kathleen twisted around and looked at Terryl. "You're very quiet. Aren't you hungry?"

Terryl shrugged.

"She's still thinking about Uncle Mark's violin playing," said Pam.

"It was so beautiful," said Terryl breathlessly.

"It was," agreed David. "My brother is a wonderful musician, and I'm proud of him. He's having dinner with us so you'll have a chance to tell him how much you enjoyed it, Terryl."

"He is? That's great!" Terryl leaned back with a smile and watched out her window as they drove toward Grand Rapids. Maybe Sunday wasn't such a bad thing after all.

TEN
The Ice Storm

Terryl shivered in the sudden burst of November rain as she ran through the school yard toward the door. The first days of school at Thornapple Elementary school last September had been the worst days she'd had in a long time. She had wanted to go back to Sunday and dinner at the Grand Plaza with Mark across the table from her, smiling and talking about music.

She bumped into Dani, then backed away and shrugged out of her jacket. "That was a short recess," she said as she hung her jacket beside Pam's.

"We can play in the gym." Dani pointed down the hall toward the gym. "Or Mrs. Haycock will let us go to our room to read or work on our Science Project."

Terryl looked around for Pam and finally found her talking to two other fourth grade girls. Terryl's stomach tightened. The new school hadn't bothered Pam at all when they'd walked in last September for the first time. She had met new friends right away. Terryl, however, had been reluctant to talk to the others in the class. She'd hated it that Mom had forced them to dress differently so that everyone could tell them apart. Everyone knew that she was Terryl Tyler and they probably were wondering why she was so quiet and so dumb. Mrs. Haycock had asked her questions during reading and she'd choked right up without being able to answer. She couldn't understand herself; Pam always had been the backward twin. *What's wrong with me?* Terryl wondered gloomily.

"What do you want to do, Terryl?" asked Dani, nudging her arm.

"I guess go to the gym," she said.

Dani led the way, motioning for Pam to follow. Dani's blonde curls bobbed as she ran into the gym and scooped up a red four-square ball. "We'll play four-square."

"I get to be server," called Terryl as she ran toward the server's square. She caught the ball and stood behind the server line and waited for Pam, Dani, and a girl named Hallie Lincoln to get into place. Terryl squared her shoulders. She would keep the server's square and no one would take it from her!

"Let's start!" called Dani, jumping inside her square.

Pam watched Terryl bounce the ball, then scoop up with her arms and strike under the ball with her palms. Pam's stomach tightened nervously—she was always the first one out in four-square.

The ball went high into the air and came straight down in Dani's square. It hit and bounced up high again. Dani waited, her hands ready. She hit it to Hallie's square and Hallie hit it to Pam's. To Pam's surprise she hit the ball to Dani without missing.

Just then Sarah James ran into the gym shouting, "The principal just announced that school's dismissed. An ice storm is making the roads icy!" She jumped up and down and shouted louder and her round face turned red. Her shirt pulled apart from her jeans, showing pink skin. "School's out! School's out!"

Terryl let the ball bounce away as she ran with the others out the gym door toward the classroom. She'd rather be at the ranch with Malcom anyway than in this new school with all the strangers staring at her. She dropped to her seat and waited.

Mrs. Haycock held up her hand for silence. A worried frown wrinkled her forehead and she pushed back her gray hair with an unsteady hand. "Children, children, please be quiet! This is a very serious matter. The rain is already freezing on the streets, making driving hazardous. You must be quiet now and listen to me."

Terryl's heart skipped a beat, then raced on. She folded her hands on her desk and leaned forward.

Mrs. Haycock walked around her desk and stood in front of it, waiting until there was total silence in the room. In the hallway lockers slammed and children talked in hushed tones. "Boys and girls, I want you to get your coats and then file to the buses quickly and quietly without pushing and shoving. We want to get you home as soon as possible before the storm hits harder. Listen to your radio in the morning to see if school is cancelled. You are dismissed."

Terryl shot from her seat, looking across the room

for Pam. Pam would be frightened about the ice storm. Everything frightened Pam. Terryl frowned, thinking, *At least that's how it used to be.*

In the hall Pam pushed Terryl's jacket into her arms. "Hurry, Terryl. We don't want to miss the bus." Butterflies fluttered in Pam's stomach. She didn't want to think about ice all over everything. She'd heard about the ice storm one year that had broken down trees and electric wires so that people for miles around had no electricity, and she didn't want it to happen now.

When they got outside, cold rain slashed against the twins as they followed close behind Dani to the bus. They pushed inside and sat toward the middle of the bus, too frightened to talk or move.

Finally the bus pulled out, the driver gripping the steering wheel tightly. While in town the bus stayed on the streets without slipping, but once outside the city limits, the road looked like solid ice. The windshield wipers clicked noisily back and forth on the windshield, forcing the freezing rain off. The back of the bus fishtailed and Terryl gasped and locked her icy hands in her lap. She saw Pam's face grow pale and she knew hers was doing the same.

"Don't worry, girls," whispered Dani. "We have angels watching over us. We'll be all right."

"I hope so," said Pam in a small voice. She had heard that God sent angels to watch over his children, but she didn't know if it was true or not. Still, Dani seemed to believe it.

Terryl stared out the window, shivering even in the warmth of the bus as the ice froze against the window. She held her breath as the bus stopped to let off several boys and girls. The tires spun and then caught hold as the bus pulled forward again. Each time it stopped Terryl wondered if it would be able to get started again. Did the driver really know what he was doing? Would he be able to deliver everyone home safely?

Just then the bus fishtailed again, and the back tire dropped suddenly into a ditch. The bus wouldn't move—it was stuck. The few children left in the bus pressed their faces against the windows to look out, exclaiming in horror about the situation.

"What'll happen now?" wailed Pam, her heart racing. "We might sit here and freeze to death!"

Dani shook her head. "Don't worry. Everything will work out OK."

Terryl frowned. How could Dani be so sure?

The bus driver clicked open the door and stepped out into the cold rain. Terryl watched as he hunched his shoulders and walked around to investigate the situation. He shook his head and her heart sank. He ran to the door and climbed inside, shutting out the freezing rain.

"Kids, sit down again and be patient. When I see a car coming, I'll flag it down for help. We'll be out of here soon. You'll see." He pushed his cap to the back of his dark head and sat on his seat, watching for a passing motorist.

"Dad will come," Dani said firmly. "I know he will."

Terryl shivered. She knew her dad wouldn't think about what time they got home. Both she and Pam carried door keys on chains around their necks to let themselves in after school. Most of the time they were home alone for an hour. But David was different. All the Keyes were. Someone was always home. Dani never had to stay alone or get home from school and let herself in. Maybe Dani was right and David would drive up in his pickup or station wagon or car and get them.

"It's too slippery for David to come after us," whispered Pam. She had watched other cars slip and slide as they had left the school earlier.

"He'll come." Dani nodded. "He'll come no matter how slick the roads are."

Just then a car stopped and the bus driver climbed out and talked to the driver. Soon he was back inside. "Mr. Clayton said he'd call someone to get us out and he's going to call your parents to tell them about the difficulty." He picked up a bag near his seat and walked back to the handful of children. "Here. I have apples. Help yourselves."

Terryl managed a thank you as she took an apple and passed the bag to Pam. Terryl bit into the juicy apple and it relieved the dryness in her throat.

For a while the only sounds were crunching and the beat of rain against the windows. Then a sob from the back of the bus tore through the silence and everyone turned to see Sarah James crying into her shaking hands.

The driver walked slowly, carefully back to her and led her to the front. "You'll be all right, Sarah. I've gotten you home safely before, haven't I?"

"But you never went in the ditch before." Her round shoulders shook with sobs and her voice cracked.

"That tire in the ditch doesn't hurt a flea. It just

keeps us from driving. Mr. Clayton will have help to us sooner than you can sneeze."

Someone sneezed and everyone laughed. Car lights flashed through the rain and everyone ran to windows to look out.

"It's Dad!" cried Dani. "I told you he'd come! Didn't I say that? I told you!"

Soon David stood on the bus steps, filling the space with his size. He smiled at the girls. "Anyone want a ride home, or is this a picnic?"

Dani ran to David and hugged him while Terryl and Pam walked slowly down the aisle. Pam wanted to rush to him and feel his strong arms around her, but she hung back until he released Dani.

Dani looked up at David. "Could we give Sarah James a ride?"

David nodded. "And the Peters kids too. I talked to their parents." He waved his hand. "Come on, gang. Let's load up in my bus and head out. Be careful walking. It's slick and wet out there."

The cold wind and rain hit Terryl and almost took her breath away. She balanced carefully, her head down and her hands out as she slipped and slid toward the station wagon. She caught the open door and held on tightly while she waited for the Peters children to climb in. Finally she slid into the car and dropped onto the seat in relief, shivering with cold, her hair dripping.

Suddenly she realized Pam was not directly behind her as she'd thought. She peered through the window with narrow eyes and her heart raced with alarm. As she watched she saw David with his arm snuggly around Pam walk to the car. He eased her inside and wiped water from her face. Anger rushed through Terryl and she bit back harsh words. David had no business touching Pam, but he acted as if he had every right.

"Are you all right now, Pam?" asked David tenderly.

Pam nodded. "My leg hurts a little."

"What happened to you?" asked Terryl sharply.

"I fell, but David picked me up and helped me to the car." Pam looked at David as he slid under the steering wheel. "He's so strong! David, you're so strong!"

"That's our dad," said Dani proudly, patting his shoulder as he slowly drove away from the bus. "He's the best dad in the world!"

David grinned and winked. "Thanks. I'm glad you think so."

Sarah James huddled against the door with Terryl beside her. "I think he's ugly," whispered Sarah. "Don't you?"

Terryl nodded. She lifted her chin defiantly and said, "My dad is the best dad in the entire universe! Pam and I both think so. Don't we, Pam?" Terryl jabbed Pam's arm and Pam sank lower in her seat. Terryl pressed her lips tightly together and leaned back with her arms crossed over her thin chest.

Inch by inch David drove along the icy road. He helped the Peters children into their house, then drove Sarah home. She walked away without a thank you or a smile.

"She's jealous," whispered Dani. "Her dad never pays any attention to her so she's jealous of Dad and us."

"David's wonderful," said Pam with a long sigh.

Terryl reached up and jerked on Pam's hair. Pam let out a shriek and turned to glare at Terryl. Before they could speak David slipped back into the car and drove across the road to their long driveway.

"Your mother will be glad to see you girls," said David. "Icy roads scare her."

"Nothing scares you, does it, David?" Pam smiled at him and he smiled back. It made Terryl sick to her stomach.

She walked toward the house, her face set. No way would she let David get to her the way he had Pam and Dani. Just then, Terryl slipped and caught herself. With a shiver she walked in the back door and was met by the smell of hot cocoa. David walked up to her quietly.

"I love you, Terryl," he whispered for her ears alone.

She jerked away from him and pulled off her jacket, her heart racing. Why couldn't they just leave her alone? Why did everyone have to talk so much about love? Terryl shivered again, and wondered how she would ever survive the rest of her nine months with these strange people.

ELEVEN
The Terrible Fight

For the next several days Terryl stayed as far away from David as she could. No way would she let him know what a hero he was. Besides, Pam seemed to be singing his praises every second and Terryl was not going to join in.

"You hear that, Malcom?" Terryl hugged the big dog. "I won't fall all over David the way Pam does. And he better never again tell me that he loves me!"

Once again the soft words that David had spoken curled around her heart and she frowned and shook her head. He couldn't really love her; she hadn't given him the chance to.

A horse whinnied in the pasture, and a tractor drove past on the road that was finally free from the ice that had closed the school for three days.

Terryl walked slowly around the corner of the house, then abruptly stopped when she saw Pam and David sitting on the porch steps talking. Anger rushed through Terryl and she wanted to grab Pam and run with her back to Dad in Detroit. How dare Pam forget all about Dad and turn to David as if *he* was her dad?

Terryl crept behind bushes so that she could listen

to Pam and David without being seen. Terryl doubled her fists and pressed her lips tightly together. Pam was going to be very sorry for caring for David!

"I know Jesus loves me," Pam said softly as she looked down at her hands. "I want to be a Christian, but I don't know how to go about it."

David hugged her close and Terryl bit back an angry cry. "Pam, just ask Jesus to be your Savior," he said. "We'll pray right now if you want."

"I do want." Pam dabbed tears from her eyes as she bowed her head. "Jesus, I love you and I know you love me. I want to belong to you. I want you as my Lord and Savior."

Terryl's stomach fluttered and a funny feeling spread through her as Pam and then David prayed.

Pam lifted her head and smiled. "I'm a Christian now, David, and I'm so happy! I feel new!"

"You have a new spirit, Pam. Your old nature is dead and a new spirit is in its place. You belong to God now, and I'm glad. I know your mother will want to hear all about it. Shall we go find her and tell her?" David stood up, towering over Pam. Terryl wanted to yell for him to mind his own business and leave Pam alone, but she bit back the words and crouched lower until the door slammed behind them.

Slowly she walked away with Malcom beside her. "What will I do now, Malcom? Pam won't even seem like my twin now."

Terryl stopped short and her eyes widened as a plan formed in her mind, a plan that was so terrible

that it might get them sent packing back to Dad.
She giggled and clapped and danced a little jig in
the grass beside Malcom. He looked at her and
barked. "I will tell you later, Malcom. You stay here
until I come back."

Terryl stepped inside the back door and waited,
her ears open to every sound. Soft music drifted
from the kitchen along with smells of freshly baked
bread. Her stomach growled and she sucked it in
until it quit. Voices drifted through the house, but
she couldn't tell which room they came from.
Silently she ran down the hall to the stairs. It was
almost time to get washed and changed for supper,
so she knew Pam would be up soon.

Terryl's skin tingled with excitement and a little
fear as she opened Pam's door and slipped inside
the ugly purple room. She wrinkled her nose and
poked out her tongue. "Yuk!"

After several minutes had passed the door opened
and Pam ran in. Her face glowed with happiness
and Terryl felt a momentary pang of guilt over what
she was going to do.

"Hi, Terryl. What're you doing in here? Mom said
to hurry and clean up for supper. She was looking
all over for you."

"Oh? Is she outdoors?"

"Yes." Pam tugged off the soiled tee shirt and
flung it into the basket in the corner of the room.

"How about David? Where is he?"

"In the family room listening to music. He's ready
for supper." Pam kicked her jeans into the basket
and reached for a clean pair. "You'd better hurry,

97

Terryl." Pam looked around for her shoes. Terryl saw them poking out from under the bed and she ran to stand in front of them so Pam couldn't see them.

"What're you looking for, Pam?" How innocent she sounded!

"My shoes."

"I remember seeing them in Dani's room. I think you left them there last night when we were watching TV with her." Terryl crossed her fingers behind her back as she said the lie.

"Thanks, Terryl. See you downstairs." Pam ran out the door and Terryl ducked down and pushed the shoes under the bed farther.

In a flash Terryl dressed in Pam's dirty shirt and jeans, then raced down the stairs to the family room. The music filled the hallway as she stopped to catch her breath. Slowly she walked inside. David sat with his long legs out and his head back, listening to Chopin. The beauty of the music almost stopped Terryl, but she stiffened her back and cleared her throat.

David sat up, pulling his long legs in. He smiled. "Hello, Pam. I thought you went up to change."

Terryl twisted her fingers together like she'd seen Pam do thousands of times. "David, I had to come talk to you."

"Sure. Sit down." He patted the arm of his chair and she hesitated, then walked to the couch and sat facing him. She didn't dare try to sit close to him or she'd give herself away.

"David, I came to tell you that I was just teasing you a while ago when I said I wanted to be a

Christian. I didn't mean it at all when I prayed."

David studied her thoughtfully as he fingered his beard. "I'm sorry to hear that. But why would you tease about such a thing?"

"Terryl dared me to do it, so I decided to fake it. But I felt so bad that I had to come tell you the truth. I don't want to be a Christian until I talk to Dad first. He might not like it. I love him and I don't want to do anything to hurt him."

David shook his head. "I don't believe you."

Terryl's head shot up. "What? How come? You have to believe me!"

"I don't know why you're doing this, but I know what I know."

Terryl jumped up, her eyes flashing. "You don't know anything! I don't want to be a Christian and I don't want anything more to do with you. You were so brave in the ice storm and so good about rescuing me that I got carried away. You can understand that, can't you?"

David slowly pushed himself up and walked around the coffee table to stand over her. "Why are you doing this?"

Terryl shrugged.

David reached down and lifted her to her feet. His touch burned into her arm and she tried to pull away, but his grip tightened. "I want to know the truth, Terryl!"

She gasped and blinked in surprise. "Why are you calling me Terryl? I'm Pam, and you know it."

"No. I know that you're Terryl and you're playing with fire. Now, tell me what's going on inside that head of yours." David's blue eyes bored into hers and she ducked her head to get away from his piercing gaze.

Gently he cupped his large hand under her chin and tipped up her face so that she was forced to look at him. "Why are you doing this, Terryl?"

Before she could answer Pam walked into the room and stopped dead. "Terryl! Why are you wearing my clothes?" First confusion, then anger crossed her face. "Are you pretending to be me?" she demanded.

"It's all right, Pam," said David. "I'll take care of it. You find your mother and tell her we'll be a little late to supper."

"It is *not* all right!" cried Pam, running to Terryl's side. "You tell me right now what terrible trick you're playing!" Pam's dark eyes smoldered and her cheeks flushed red. "Tell me right now, Terryl!"

Terryl looked around in panic. She was trapped between Pam and David, the couch, and the coffee table. She turned on Pam in a rage. "It's all your fault, Pamela! I told you that we were here to get Mom and Dad back together, but you forgot all about that, didn't you? You want to be a Christian and you want David for a father instead of Dad! Well, you can't have your own way. Do you hear me?"

Pam trembled and the color drained from her face. She opened her mouth to speak, but couldn't.

"Girls, you are not going to fight about this," said David sternly. "We'll sit down and discuss it without yelling."

"I won't!" cried Terryl.

The lump dissolved from Pam's throat. "Oh, yes you will, Terryl Ann Tyler! And you won't dress like me again to make trouble for me!"

Terryl stared at Pam in shock.

"You won't push me around another day, Terryl! I happen to love David and I like it that he's my new stepfather. And you can't change my mind no matter what you do or say!" Pam couldn't believe that she'd found the courage to speak up to Terryl. It felt wonderful, and a little scary because she knew Terryl wouldn't forget it.

The music stopped and the silence suddenly seemed louder than the shouting and the music. A door slammed somewhere in the house and Dani called to Diane.

"Both of you girls sit down and we'll discuss this rationally." David clamped one hand around Pam's arm and another around Terryl's and sat them on the couch side by side. He sat on the coffee table with his knees almost touching his beard. "You girls are not going to fight. You're going to talk and come to some sort of agreement."

Terryl flipped back, crossed her arms, and poked out her chin stubbornly. She wouldn't talk no matter what David said or did.

Pam leaned back and pressed her lips tightly together. She wouldn't speak to Terryl until Terryl apologized for the terrible thing she'd tried to do.

David sighed and shook his head. "So, is this the way you girls are going to act? You can't spend the rest of your time here fighting. How can we settle this?"

"We can go back to Dad!" Terryl's eyes narrowed

as she watched to see how David took that. He
didn't bat an eye or twitch a muscle.

"I won't go," said Pam in a strained voice. "I want
to stay with Mom and David."

Terryl flung herself against Pam and pounded
against her with her fists until David bodily lifted
her off and held her under his arm, kicking and
screaming. Terryl's throat ached with the loud
screams, but she screamed harder.

"Stop it this minute, Terryl!" he snapped. He
stood her to the floor and gripped her shoulders. "I
mean it! Stop that screaming!"

Pam huddled in the corner of the couch, sobbing
into her hands. Right now she hated Terryl, and she
didn't want her for a sister.

Kathleen ran in, her face white. "What is going on
in here, David? Why are the twins so upset?"

Terryl broke away from David and flung herself
against Kathleen. "He's being mean to us, Mom! He
hates us and he just wants to make us miserable!"

Kathleen frowned in concern. "David, what
happened?"

David and Pam both looked at her in surprise.
"Kathleen, I didn't do anything to them," David said
firmly. "Be careful what you believe." He strode out
and Terryl hid a pleased smile.

Kathleen led Terryl to the couch and she sat down
between the twins. "I want to hear what happened,
girls. I want the truth."

"I told the truth," said Terryl sharply.

"No, you didn't!" cried Pam. "David wasn't mean
to us. Terryl started everything."

"Me? I did not!" Terryl faked a few tears. "Mom, I

didn't do anything. I promise. I didn't." Terryl ignored the coldness in her heart. Somehow she had to convince Mom to take them back to Dad. "You do believe me, don't you, Mom?"

Kathleen pulled the girls close. "We'll talk about it later. Diane has supper ready."

"I don't want to eat," said Pam miserably.

"I'll never eat again," said Terryl. She could picture herself growing thinner and thinner until she vanished away. Maybe then Mom and Dad would be sorry for ruining their lives. Her stomach growled with hunger. By tomorrow at this time she'd probably be a little skeleton that everyone would feel sorry for. A tear slipped down her pale cheek and she let it fall.

TWELVE
The Missing
Photograph

Dani raced across the yard, sliding to a stop beside Terryl who was putting Malcom inside the kennel for the night. Dani grabbed Terryl's arm and jerked her around. "How dare you be so mean to Dad? I just heard your mom arguing with Dad because of you. You're mean, Terryl Tyler. Mean and hateful!"

"I agree with that," said Sarah James with a laugh as she came up and stopped beside the girls. "I came to play and I'm not going home no matter what."

Terryl leaned wearily against the kennel fence. She was tired from a full day of school, and the fight with David and Pam, and the long, long talk with Mom. She didn't want to put up with Sarah James. "Play all you want, Sarah. I'm going inside to watch TV."

"So?" Sarah shrugged her plump shoulders. "I'll watch too."

Dani shook her head. "No way! I am going to talk with Terryl and you are going home, Sarah. I mean it. We'll play tomorrow after school."

"I'll tell your dad on you!"

"It won't do any good, Sarah. He won't want you here tonight either."

Sarah tapped her toe in the grass. "I wonder if your dad was this mean when he had a fight with your new mom?"

Dani's face flamed. "Go home, Sarah, and I mean it!"

Terryl pushed Sarah back. "You get out of this yard before I sic Malcom on you."

Sarah screamed and ran for home. Half way down the drive she turned and shouted, "I hate you, Tyler twin! You're ugly and so is your sister!" Sarah spun around and ran.

"You didn't have to do that," said Dani. "She would've gone home without you scaring her so much."

"She's stupid." Terryl watched Malcom walk to his dog dish and lap up water. She didn't want to face Dani and listen to any angry words from her.

Dani pushed her fingers through her blonde curls. "Terryl, you lied about Dad! He would never do anything to hurt you or Pam, and you know that. But now your mom is yelling at Dad and making him feel bad. I wish your mom hadn't married my dad!"

Terryl blinked in surprise. "How can you say that? There's nothing wrong with Mom."

Dani twisted her toe in the grass as she shoved her hands into her jeans pockets. "She's not like *my* mom. She used to sing all the time. Kathleen can't carry a tune. And my mom did things with me all the time."

Terryl tugged down her shirt. "Mom does things with us all the time. She *is* nice, Dani. I can't understand why you don't think so."

Dani frowned. "I think she's nice and I do like her, but she isn't Mom. She's a stranger in our house and she's married to Dad. Sometimes I think he's forgotten all about Mom and thinks only about Kathleen. He really loves her . . . and now she's yelling at him because of your lies. It's just not fair!"

To Terryl's surprise Dani burst into tears. Terryl didn't know what to do or what to say. She had never thought of Dani's side of things. Tears stung Terryl's eyes and she blinked them away. "Why don't you tell David to kick Mom and us out and then we can go back to live with Dad and be a family."

"Oh, you can't be that dumb, can you?" Dani stamped her small foot. "Dad and Kathleen are married and they will never get a divorce. They promised each other that. Nothing you will do or say will make them break up, but it will make them unhappy. And I don't want Dad to be unhappy. He was sad for a long, long time after Mom died. When he met Kathleen and fell in love with her, I told him that I would try to love her, too. It wasn't hard to live with her . . . not until you came and spoiled everything."

"Me?" Terryl pointed to herself in surprise. "It's your dad! He goes around saying he loves everyone. He sure can't love me when I have my own dad. What would my dad say if suddenly he found out that I had another dad to love?"

"You make life so hard, Terryl. What's wrong with loving two dads? At least your dad is alive so that you *can* love him. My mom is dead." Dani sniffed and rubbed her hand across her nose. "Her body is dead and is buried at the cemetery and her spirit is

107

alive and lives in heaven with Jesus. So, she really is alive; she just lives somewhere else where I can't see her or talk to her. You should be glad that you can talk to your dad on the phone and write to him and live with him three months out of the year."

That kind of thinking was so new to Terryl that she knew she'd have to sit down quietly and decide how she felt about it. She *was* glad that Dad was alive and living in Detroit, and that Mom was alive, too. Even if they could never live together again, they were still alive. "I'm going to my room," she said stiffly.

"You tell Dad you're sorry first, Terryl. And you tell your mom that Dad didn't do anything to hurt you." Dani grabbed Terryl's arm and tugged, but Terryl broke free and shook her head.

"No way, Dani! You go tell them if you want, but I won't do it." Terryl couldn't stand to think about embarrassing herself that way. She ran away from Dani and didn't stop until she was inside her beautiful bedroom.

She pushed the door closed and let the cheerful colors soothe her. Slowly she walked across the room to pick up the photograph of Dad to talk to him. With a cry she dropped down beside the night-stand and stared at the empty spot where once the picture had stood. "Where is it? Who took it?" She rubbed the empty spot as if to make the picture appear, but it didn't. Who would be so mean? Surely not David or Mom. Dani? Could Dani have done this? Terryl shook her head.

"Sarah James," she cried. Sarah was the only

mean person around and she could've easily sneaked into the room to take the picture.

Terryl raced downstairs, but before she could reach the door Kathleen grabbed her arm and stopped her. Terryl struggled. "Let me go. I have to get Sarah James right now!"

"You're not going anywhere, young lady, until we have a long talk." Kathleen's face was set with determination and Terryl almost wept with frustration.

"We'll talk later, Mom. Please let me go find Sarah first."

"No!" Kathleen dragged Terryl to the family room and pushed her toward David who stood in front of the stone fireplace. Kathleen looked up at David. "Terryl is ready to apologize for lying."

Terryl's stomach cramped painfully and her mouth went dry.

"Go ahead, Terryl," said Kathleen grimly. "I want you to apologize."

"But I told you the truth," said Terryl stubbornly.

David looked at her without saying a word and she dropped her gaze to stare at the thick carpet.

"Terryl, I know David," said Kathleen. "I was upset for a while, but when I stopped to think clearly, I knew he wouldn't be unkind to you girls. If he did punish you for something, then he'd tell me about it. Your accusations caused us all problems, and I want you to apologize."

Terryl suddenly realized that it was getting dark outdoors and that if she didn't get out of here now she'd have to wait until tomorrow to see Sarah and get the photograph back. "I'm sorry, David. I shouldn't have pretended to be Pam and I shouldn't have lied."

"You could be a little more sincere," said Kathleen impatiently.

"It's all right," said David. "I can see that Terryl has something on her mind right now. She and I will talk later when she has more time. Right, Terryl?"

Terryl stared at David as if he'd suddenly turned blue. How could he read her mind that way? Finally she nodded. "I am sorry," she whispered, and she really meant it. She spun around and ran from the room and to the front door.

A few minutes later she stood outside Sarah's front door, knocking hard and gasping for breath. From inside the small yellow house she heard the TV and knocked again.

Finally the door opened and Sarah stood there. She blinked in surprise. "What're you doing here? Nobody's supposed to come over when I'm home all alone."

"I came to get back the picture of my dad." Terryl pushed her way into the cluttered living room. She looked around, but couldn't see the picture. "Where did you put it? Did you hide it in your room?"

Sarah grabbed Terryl's shirt and tugged. "You get out of here. My dad will get mad if he knows I let you in the house. Get out right now!"

Terryl broke free and faced Sarah angrily. "I'll leave as soon as you give me back the picture of my dad that you took off my nightstand in my bedroom."

Sarah flounced around, her hands on her hips. "I've never been in your dumb old room, twin! And I wouldn't want to take your dumb old picture of your dumb old dad."

Terryl sank back against a big chair covered with clothes. For some reason she believed Sarah. "If you didn't take it, who did?"

"Don't ask me, twin. Now, will you get out of here before my dad gets home and sees you?" Sarah pushed Terryl toward the open door.

Slowly Terryl walked away from the small yellow house. She looked both ways and crossed the road to the drive that led to the huge house on the Big Key, frowning thoughtfully as she walked. Who had taken her picture? She'd have to ask everyone in the house and make the guilty person return it to her. Her short legs pumped up and down as she ran toward the lighted ranch house.

THiRTEEN
Broken Plants

Terryl burst into her bedroom, panting for breath. She looked to make sure the photograph really was gone and that she hadn't just imagined it. The corners of her mouth drooped when she saw the empty nightstand. It was gone all right and someone in this house had taken it. But why?

Pam! Maybe Pam had wanted to have it in her room for a while to look at so that she'd remember what Dad looked like.

Terryl dashed across the hall and into Pam's room. Pam looked up from reading a book at her desk. "Pam, where is it?"

Pam frowned. "What're you talking about?"

"The picture of Dad. I thought you might have it so you could look at it to remind you of him." Terryl looked around frantically, but didn't see it. Her heart sank, and she turned and dashed out.

Pam sighed in relief. Terryl must never learn the truth about the picture. If she did, no one would be able to live happily in this house.

Dani knocked and walked in. "I saw Terryl run past my room. Did she find out yet?"

"About the picture?"

Dani nodded and rubbed her hands down her jeans.

"Terryl would never forgive me if she knew that I broke the frame and ruined the picture." Pam said, pacing across the room and back, rubbing her hands in agitation. "I should tell Mom. She'll know what to do."

"I saw her working in the greenhouse just a few minutes ago." Dani didn't tell Pam about her fight with Terryl. Poor Pam didn't need any more worries.

"Terryl will probably tear through the house and accuse everyone. She won't calm down until she has her picture back." Pam's voice rose. "And that can't happen! Oh, dear! Why didn't I take my anger out on something else?"

Pam dropped to the edge of her bed and tucked her honey-brown hair behind her ears. "I'll tell Mom when she comes in to say good night. She'll know how to handle Terryl. I just hope we all live through this!" Pam flung herself back on her bed and stared up at the ceiling. A round circle of light glowed softly on the ceiling from the lamp beside her bed. "I wish Terryl would learn to love David so we could all be happy here."

Dani perched on the edge of the chair near the desk. "You love Dad, don't you, Pam?"

Pam sat up and nodded. "I'm glad he's our dad. He is super! My dad is moody and snaps at me a lot because I don't like to read or play a violin. I love him because he is my dad, but it's nice to have another dad to love."

"Do you ever feel guilty about loving him?"

Pam shook her head. "Terryl wants me to, but I

don't. I know how to love a lot of people. Terryl thinks I should have only enough love for Mom and Dad and her. But she's wrong!"

Dani picked at her fingernail. "I wish I could learn to love your mom more. But I start remembering mine and then I can't love Kathleen the way Dad wants me to."

"Maybe you don't have to love her the way you loved your mom. I love David in a different way than I love Dad. Maybe you love my mom in another way."

Dani thought about that for a while and then nodded. "You know what? I think you're right!" Her blue eyes sparkled once again and she jumped up. "You really helped me a lot, Pam. Thanks."

Pam puffed out with pride. She couldn't remember ever helping anyone before. "What are sisters for, except to help each other?"

Dani grinned. "We *are* sisters, and I'm glad."

"Yeah, me too. I just wish Terryl would feel the same way." Pam sighed heavily.

Outdoors Terryl ran toward the greenhouse to find Mom. Diane had said that Mom had gone out to close up for the night to keep the tender plants from getting too cold. Mom had always wanted a greenhouse to grow her own vegetables and flowers. Now she had one. With the ranch and David and the animals and the greenhouse, Terryl knew Mom would never want to leave the Big Key.

Terryl stopped in the middle of the sidewalk as the realization hit her—no matter what she did, Mom was here to stay. Mom belonged here and not in an apartment in Detroit with a man she didn't love.

Terryl wrapped her arms across herself and moaned. A cool breeze blew country smells to her and she sniffed deeply. This was much better than city smells that choked her. Maybe it was time to stop fighting and start enjoying her stay on the Big Key. If she tried, maybe she could learn to like David. She'd never love him since he wasn't Dad and never would be, but maybe she could like him a little without feeling guilty.

She nodded slightly. Just as soon as she found out who had taken the picture of Dad, she'd start fresh with David. She'd stop avoiding him and she'd talk to him when he talked to her. A heavy weight lifted off her and she ran lightly to the greenhouse door just as Mom stepped out.

"Terryl!" Kathleen grabbed her arm. Tears clung to Kathleen's dark lashes. "How could you be so destructive? I couldn't save any of the marigolds and only a few of the tomatoes."

Terryl frowned. "What do you mean, Mom?"

"You know what I mean. You're the only one angry enough at me to do this damage."

"I'm not mad at you, Mom." Terryl's stomach tightened; she was becoming frightened.

"Then why did you do this?" Kathleen held Terryl's arm and led her back inside the greenhouse. She turned the lights back on and pointed. "This sure didn't happen by itself!"

Terryl looked at the soil and plants flung around the flats and onto the concrete floor. She shook her head numbly. "I didn't do it, Mom. Honest, I didn't!" Just then she thought about Dani and their fight and she gasped. Dani must have done this to get back at her as well as Mom! But would Dani do such a mean thing since she was a Christian?

Kathleen sniffed and wipped tears from her eyes. "I don't know what to do about you, Terryl. I know the divorce is hard on you, but I thought once you saw how happy I am, you'd feel better about it."

"I do, Mom. I know you fit right in to this place."

"Did you realize that before or after this destruction?" Kathleen asked drily.

Terryl's face flamed. "I didn't do this, Mom!"

Just then David walked in. His eyes widened as he looked around. "What happened in here?"

Kathleen clung to him and he wrapped his long arms around her. "My plants have been ruined!" she said tearfully.

David frowned at Terryl. "What do you have to say about this, young lady? Was this your doing?"

Frustration welled up inside her and she shook her head. Tears glistened in her eyes. "No! Honest! I came out here to talk to Mom." Suddenly she remembered about the picture and she clenched her fists. "Someone took the picture of Dad out of my room and I want it back! I came to get you to help me, Mom."

Kathleen turned on Terryl and anger darkened her eyes. "I don't want to see or hear about that picture. You've just used it to avoid learning to love David, or to enjoy living here with us. I'm glad it's gone!"

"Kathleen, don't." David rubbed her arms with his sun-darkened hands.

Terryl backed away from her mother, her eyes wide with shock. She'd seen Mom lose her temper before, but she'd never been so angry that she'd said anything like this. Kathleen turned from David, her face sad and tear-stained.

"I'm sorry, David!" she said quietly. "But Terryl just can't accept that we're a family. Maybe it would be better if she went to live with Richard." Kathleen turned back to Terryl. "Is that what you want, Terryl?"

Terryl hesitated. That *was* what she wanted, wasn't it? But only if Mom and Pam would go with her. When she didn't respond, her mom shook her head sadly.

"All right, Terryl. We'll send you back to Richard," said Kathleen in a dead voice. "You can leave tomorrow on the first flight."

Terryl stood still a moment, then pushed past Mom and David and ran into the night, her head buzzing. Tomorrow she'd be with Dad. But instead of being happy, tears filled her eyes and a great loneliness swept over her.

fOURTEEN
Happy Family

Terryl burst into Dani's room. "Why did you do it, Dani? You're a Christian and I didn't think you'd do anything really bad." Terryl's chest rose and fell as she gasped for breath after running at top speed from the greenhouse.

Dani slid off her bed and stood up. Her quilted bathrobe brushed her small bare feet, and she looked at Terryl, confused. "What do you mean?"

"You know very well what I mean!"

"Are you talking about your Dad's picture? I know it's broken and I'm sorry."

Terryl blinked, then her eyes widened and she cried, "It's broken? The picture of Dad is broken?"

Before Dani could speak Pam walked in. Butterflies fluttered in her stomach and she moistened her dry lips with the tip of her tongue. "Don't yell at Dani, Terryl. She didn't have anything to do with breaking the picture. I did it."

Terryl fell back, her hand to her heart. It was hard to speak around the lump in her throat. "You did it, Pam? But why would you take Dad's picture?"

Her cheeks flamed. "I was mad, Terryl. I wanted you to like it here and I wanted you to like David, but you wouldn't give him a chance. I picked up the picture of Dad and slammed it down. When the glass broke a piece poked into the picture and ruined it. I threw it all away and then pretended nothing had happened. I am sorry, Terryl. I'll get you another picture."

Helplessly Terryl shook her head. Did she know Pam at all? "It doesn't matter," she said tonelessly. "I'm going home tomorrow anyway."

"But you are home," said Dani with a puzzled look.

"Home to Dad, to Detroit."

Pam gasped and shook her head. "No! No, I won't go! I mean it, Terryl! I am staying right here with Mom and David."

Terryl felt cold inside. "You don't have to go, Pam. Mom's sending me away because she thinks I wrecked her plants." Terryl faced Dani helplessly. "You know I didn't ruin her plants, don't you? You did it, because you were mad at Mom." Dani looked at her, shocked.

"Me? I didn't do anything! How can you say that?"

Terryl's head drooped and she walked toward the door. "All I know is that I didn't ruin the plants. But Mom thinks I did, and tomorrow I'm leaving the Big Key and I might never come back. I'll never get to see Mom again . . . I'll probably be doomed to stay in Detroit all the rest of my life. I didn't hurt those little plants in the greenhouse. But nobody will listen, or cares about me."

Pam and Dani looked helplessly at each other, then ran after Terryl. They watched as she slumped to her bed, her shoulders bent and her head down. Music drifted up the stairs from the family room. A faint aroma of coffee hung in the air.

Just then, Gran walked in dressed in a pale blue bathrobe tied at her narrow waist. "What's this I hear about you leaving tomorrow, Terryl?"

Terryl nodded. "It's true. I was blamed for something I didn't do." Her voice cracked. "I am being sent away, away from my very own twin."

Pam rolled her eyes. It was really embarrassing when Terryl started being so dramatic.

"Lift your head and look at me," commanded Gran. "I want to see your face when you talk to me."

Terryl's head shot up and she waited, suddenly wondering if Gran could help her.

"Now, Terryl, do you *want* to go live with your dad instead of staying here with us?" Gran stood with her hands at her waist, her elbows poking the air. "Well, speak up, girl!"

Terryl took a deep breath. "I want to stay here," she said in a rush before she could stop herself.

Pam gasped. "You do? Oh, Terryl, that's great!"

"But Mom won't let me," she said dejectedly.

Gran clicked her tongue. "Such nonsense. What have you done that could upset her enough to make you leave when you want to stay?"

"She thinks I ruined her little plants in the greenhouse, but I didn't. I really didn't, Gran! I don't know who did, but it wasn't me!"

Gran retied her belt on her bathrobe, a thoughtful look on her face. "You know, I saw that little James girl inside the greenhouse awhile ago. I was going to go send her on her way, but she ran out and headed home, so I let her go." Dani reached out to touch Terryl's arm.

"Sarah might do something that bad, if she's mad," Dani said. "Let's call her and find out."

"No!" Terryl surprised even herself when she spoke up. She cleared her throat and went on. "She'll get into a lot of trouble with her dad if she did do it. Let's wait and talk to her tomorrow. Maybe we can settle it with her so her parents won't have to find out."

Pam looked at Terryl in awe, amazed that her sister would really do something that nice. "I like that idea," whispered Pam.

"Me, too," said Dani. "If Sarah did do it, it was because we wouldn't play with her. We were all too upset to let her stay."

"That little girl needs a lot of help," said Gran with a nod. "I think it's time for the people at the Big Key to pitch in and help her. Little plants can be replaced, but little girls can't."

They talked for several minutes and then Terryl said, "But what if Mom still won't believe me?"

Gran patted Terryl's arm. "She will. She had quite a blow a while ago, but she'll get over it. Once she knows that you want to stay, she'll do everything to keep you here. Your mother loves you. She loves all of us. We're blessed to have her in the family."

"Let's go down and tell her," said Dani.

But before they could move, Kathleen walked in. Her face was scrubbed clean of makeup and her eyes and nose were red from crying. She looked around the room in surprise. "What's going on here? Is this a going away party?"

"No," whispered Terryl. "It's a welcome home party."

Gran quickly explained their suspicions concerning Sarah James and Kathleen nodded silently. "So, you can stop blaming Terryl and keep her here for the rest of her time with you," Gran concluded.

Kathleen shook her head. "I can't. Not if Terryl is determined to leave. It upsets the entire family, and I won't have that."

Terryl bit her bottom lip. "Mom . . . Mom, I want to stay. Will you let me?"

"She wants to stay!" cried Pam, flinging her arms wide the way Terryl did at her most dramatic moments. "She wants to stay right here on the Big Key!"

"I love you, Mom." Terryl tentatively reached out for Kathleen. "And I will try to love David. I promise."

Kathleen gathered Terryl close and hugged and kissed her as if she'd never let her go.

"Is this a family meeting?" asked David from the doorway. His shirt was unbuttoned and hung over his jeans. His feet were bare.

"Oh, David!" cried Kathleen, keeping her arms around Terryl. "She wants to stay after all. She doesn't want to leave."

David stepped into the room only to have Dani and Pam hurl themselves into his arms. He kept his arms around them as he looked at Terryl. "Welcome to the Big Key, Terryl."

"Thanks, David." Terryl smiled, suddenly feeling very shy. "I'll try to be good, and I won't pretend to be Pam or lie to you."

"You'd never fool me anyway, Terryl. I can always tell you girls apart. I was fooled only for a minute when you dressed in Pam's clothes."

Pam looked up thoughtfully. "How can you tell us apart, David?"

"Yes, how, Dad?" Dani echoed.

"Should I tell?" David asked, winking at Terryl.

She nodded, but he just grinned. "I'll never tell," he said. "It's my little secret."

Everyone started talking at once as Grandad walked in. He looked around with a laugh. "This is a regular family gathering, isn't it?"

"For a happy family," said Kathleen, smiling tenderly at the twins, then the others.

Terryl caught Pam's hand and squeezed it. "A happy family, Pam," she whispered, and Pam nodded in agreement.